SPARK
AND THE
LEAGUE OF URSUS

SPARK
AND THE
LEAGUE OF URSUS

ROBERT REPINO

QUIRK BOOKS

PHILADELPHIA

Copyright © 2020 by Robert Repino

Library of Congress Cataloging in Publication Data
Repino, Robert, author.
Spark and the League of Ursus / Robert Repino.
CYAC: Teddy bears—Fiction. | Toys—Fiction. | Monsters—Fiction. | Missing children—Fiction. | Video recordings—Production and direction—Fiction. | Rescues—Fiction. | Magic—Fiction.
LCC PZ7.1.R464 Sp 2020
DDC [Fic]—dc23   2019037434

ISBN: 978-1-68369-166-2

Printed in the United States of America

Typeset in Sabon

Cover design by Andie Reid
Interior Design by Molly Rose Murphy
Cover and interior illustrations by Ryan Andrews
Production management by John J. McGurk

Quirk Books
215 Church Street
Philadelphia, PA 19106
quirkbooks.com

10 9 8 7 6 5 4 3 2 1

For the dreamers

ONE

Spark rested her head on Loretta's chest, with her paw on the girl's rib cage as it rose and fell with each breath. Loretta's eyelashes fluttered, tickling Spark's fuzzy ear. Spark liked it. Teddy bears like her were meant for this. They were meant to stay with their human, their best friend, and watch over them in the darkest hours of the night. Outside, the buzzing streetlamp glowed like a phony sun. The toys on the windowsill cast shadows on the rug. And as the house settled in, as the quietest stretch of the night began, Spark saw the monster for the first time.

It began with a scratching sound, loud enough to make Spark lift her head. In the corner of the room, a blackness spread outward. The hardwood floor and painted walls rippled and sank into darkness. Then the void glowed red like the embers of a fire. The light glinted off Loretta's movie posters. Flickering shadows extended from the bookshelf and the enormous wooden desk. On top of the shelf, the sock monkey named Zed squatted with his paws over his eyes.

Spark waddled to the edge of the bed, where Loretta's feet rested under the blanket. She tried to stand tall enough to see into the portal that had formed in the wall. A shape appeared; it was a man's head, only larger, and with sharp horns curving upward above the brow. Spark crouched behind the footboard. She could make out the monster's face now. He had enormous eyes, like an owl. There were two holes above his mouth, as if the nose had been sheared off at the root. A thick chain wrapped around his collar, holding a hideous pendant: it was a human face, with leathery skin stretched tight, the eyes squinched shut. The links of the chain curled under its jaw, which hung open as if letting out an eternal scream.

The monster continued to rise, carrying with him the smell of grease and soot. A chain mail vest covered his torso. A plate of rusted armor, flecked with bits of gold, encased his shoulders, with two sharp points on either side. At his waist, the pale human skin gave way to greenish-black scales.

And then the first claw rose over the edge of the portal, followed by another, then another. Then another. Thin legs, with knobby hinges, like an insect's. The creature slithered out— half man, half scorpion. Spikes pointed from the armor along his spine. The tail ended in a two-pronged pincer the size of a pair of hedge clippers.

The monster stopped. The scant light reflected in his eyes. When they fixed on Spark's furry ears poking over the footboard, the monster squinted. There was no point hiding now. With Loretta still fast asleep behind her, Spark stood straight. Maybe this would be enough to scare the monster back into his hole.

It wasn't.

The monster leaned forward and bared his glistening teeth. He let out a long hiss. And then, impossibly fast, he climbed the wall. On the way up, one of his claws ripped the corner of a poster for *The Wizard of Oz*. And before Spark could speak, the monster hung upside down from the ceiling. Somehow, the necklace with the human face remained attached to his chest. His tail reached for the foot of the bed. The pincer snapped shut and then opened again like some meat-eating flower.

Spark trembled. She knew monsters were real. Teddy bears were meant to ward them off. The only problem was that she had never seen one until now.

The monster hissed again, and a blob of spit fell from his teeth onto the floor.

Spark tried to remember the oath: the sacred words, first spoken by the Founders of the League. Every bear needed to recite the oath in a moment like this. Doing so would chase away even the most powerful monster. As she hastily assembled the words in her mind, they grounded her. They felt magical. They *had* to work.

"I am Spark," she said. "I am the sworn protector of this house."

The monster's tail continued to slither. The pincer scraped along the bed frame.

Shaking, Spark continued. "We serve goodness and truth." Wait, was it goodness and truth, or truth and goodness?

On the bookshelf, Zed pulled his hands away from his eyes.

"We give refuge to the innocent," Spark said. "We defend the light . . . to the *final* light . . . in times of darkness. By the power bestowed upon me by the League of Ursus, I command you to be gone!"

She didn't even know what some of the words meant. "The final light"—what was that supposed to be? But Sir Reginald, the bear who taught her the oath, would have been proud that she got it all out at once. Though he would have nitpicked her mistakes. He would have told her to say it louder next time.

The monster should have run away by now. Instead, he let out a new hiss, higher pitched, which quickly dissolved into hysterical, cackling laughter.

A piercing shout rang out. Spark felt movement behind her. Loretta sat up, screaming. The monster grimaced. Spark covered her ears.

Loretta shot from the bed, whipping the covers so hard that she flung Spark into the air. The teddy bear collided with the desk and fell to the floor. Before Loretta could reach the door, it swung open. Light from the hall poured into the room. In the doorway, Dad stood bleary-eyed and unshaven, wearing a frayed T-shirt and boxer shorts. His face looked so different without his glasses.

"Dad!" Loretta said. "Dad, look! Look!"

"What?"

Spark turned to where the monster had been. But the creature was gone, the portal sealed.

"It's a dream, sweetie," Dad mumbled.

"No, it was—" Loretta stared at claw mark on the poster, her lip quivering.

"Come on," Dad said. "Nothing here. Get back in bed."

"Dad, I swear there was something in here!"

4

"I know, I know. But it's gone. And Mom and I are right next door." His tone suggested that eleven-year-old girls weren't supposed to have nightmares like this anymore.

Still shaking, Loretta climbed onto the bed.

"And look," Dad said, "you left poor Spark on the floor."

Spark lay still, a clump of brown fur, the way she always did when humans were watching. Loretta scooped her up and took her to the bed. She rolled away from Dad, her arm wrapped around Spark's neck.

"Are you okay, sweetie?" Dad asked.

"I'm fine."

She wasn't fine. Dad waited a moment before closing the door.

Loretta's heart thumped against Spark. The girl wept silently, stopping only when she gasped for air.

"I saw it," she said. "I *saw* it."

Long after a pool of tears gathered on the pillow, Loretta finally drifted off to sleep. Spark lay in the same position, waiting for the sun to rise, listening for the scratching noise.

Two

Spark needed to find Sir Reginald. He would know what to do.

Outside, the overcast sky glowed white through the window. Loretta stirred, the first sign that she would wake soon. Despite what had happened a few hours earlier, Spark tried to enjoy this quiet moment before the day began. Before this week, Loretta had not slept with her bear in years, preferring to leave Spark on the bookshelf. That was normal for an eleven-year-old. But something had changed in the last few days. Something scared her. Spark should have investigated sooner, but she was simply happy to be close to her friend again.

When the alarm clock buzzed, Loretta rubbed her face, set her feet on the floor, and placed Spark between the two pillows at the head of the bed. Wearing her pastel-blue pajamas, Loretta crept over to the corner of the room. She knelt and touched the hardwood slats and the painted drywall, the place where the portal had opened. Monsters almost never appeared in daytime, and even then, they stayed in dark places—though the one from last night was big enough to break whatever rules he wanted. Spark wanted to scream as Loretta ran her finger over the rip in the *Wizard of Oz* poster, an inch above the Cowardly Lion's tail. Definitely a claw mark, but it could easily be dismissed as something else—a shifting of the house, an accidental bump with her backpack. There were countless explanations that did not involve a monster.

Shaking her head, Loretta walked into the hall toward the bathroom. While she was gone, her cell phone buzzed on the dresser. Spark forced herself to remain still when, minutes later, Loretta returned and hastily changed into jeans and a zip-up hoodie. The girl tied her curly raven hair in a bun that sprouted from the crown of her head. Then she grabbed the phone on her way out the door.

In the next room over, Loretta's older brother Matthew was also on the move. After he put on his shoes, his footsteps became loud clonking sounds. On his way to the stairs, Matthew peeked inside Loretta's room to see if she was there. Despite the early hour, he wore jeans, a raincoat, and a ballcap. To Spark's surprise, he also wore a pair of boots. It was unusual to see Matthew ready to go so early on a Saturday morning, especially one as dreary as this.

Every time Spark saw him, it came as a shock. A year older than Loretta, Matthew was growing faster than ever. In another couple of years, he would stand taller than Mom, maybe even Dad too. Sir Reginald was proud, for he watched over Matthew in the same way that Spark watched over Loretta. The bears had a word for it. Loretta was Spark's *dusa*—her best friend, the one she was sworn to protect.

7

Once Matthew's footsteps faded, Spark rose from her seat and waved to Zed. The monkey still covered his eyes, so Spark needed to yell.

"Monkey, did you see that thing last night?"

"N-no," he stammered.

"Yes you did!"

Spark vaulted the footboard, landing on the rug. Her legs buckled, but her big butt and stubby tail broke the fall. That's what they were for.

"You're not supposed to do that!" Zed said. "What if she comes back?"

"The family's headed out somewhere," Spark said.

"Where?"

"I'm not sure. But Loretta's not coming back anytime soon."

Zed lowered his hands, but only a little.

"I need to know," Spark said. "Have you ever seen that monster before?"

"What monster?"

"*Stop* it, monkey."

"I kept my eyes closed! I didn't see anything!"

Zed would never change. He was a court jester, not a knight. Not a protector. When Loretta was a baby with wispy hair, she spent hours flicking Zed's tail and giggling, her first experience with humor and silliness. Sometimes she would doze off with his ear squeezed between her gums. He made her feel safe. But he did not actually keep her safe. That was Spark's job.

And anyway, arguing with Zed was a waste of time. Spark needed Sir Reginald. So she went to the closet, which shared a wall with Matthew's room. That was where Matthew stored Sir Reginald, having grown too old for a bear. Every night at three, Spark would take a quarter from Loretta's jar of coins and tap on the wall. On the other side, Sir Reginald would repeat the signal. Three simple taps meant that all was well, no monsters. Three at three, they called it. Five taps signaled danger, but they never got that high.

The night before, the monster had appeared *after* their check-in. Perhaps he wanted the bears to feel safe before he attacked.

This morning, when Spark tapped the wall, no one responded. She tapped again. Still nothing.

Sir Reginald was gone. At the worst possible time.

Spark stepped out of the closet in a daze. She saw no point in pretending to be calm. The monkey would see right through her.

"Is he there?" Zed asked.

"No," she said, unable to look him in the eye.

"Better take our places, then. Right?"

The League had a rule against what she was about to do: no roaming about the house when humans were around, except in an emergency. Sir Reginald trained her to do it quietly, quickly—while at the same time reminding her to *never* do it. If the parents ever saw a walking teddy bear, they would lose their minds.

None of that mattered, though. Not after last night.

"I'm going to find out what's going on here," Spark said. She headed for the door.

"Hey! You're not supposed to—"

"I'm not listening."

Zed clapped his hands. "Stop!" The monkey was not merely reciting the rules. He was terrified to be left alone.

"Listen, Zed. Sir Reginald's missing. Loretta is acting strange. She hasn't cuddled with me in years."

It felt weird to say that out loud.

"And then a monster appears out of nowhere!" she continued. "I want to know what's happening."

"Mom and Dad take care of that stuff! Sir Reginald said *they* handle it."

"Did you hear what I said? Sir Reginald isn't here."

The monkey covered his mouth, muffling his voice. "What if the monster comes back?"

"I'll be quick."

The door was cracked open a few inches, wide enough for Spark to squeeze through without moving it. The noises from the kitchen made their way upstairs. Spark heard the cupboard closing and the faucet running. Someone dropped a plate in the sink.

Spark crept down the hallway. The door to Matthew's room was shut. Spark shimmied up the frame and peeked inside the keyhole. Papers cluttered the desk, the bedsheets were tossed about, and random articles of clothing lay scattered on the floor. Spark whispered Sir Reginald's name, but did not hear a response. A clump of black fabric on the floor near the closet caught her eye. But it wasn't the bear, just a winter coat that Matthew needed to stow away for the spring.

Matthew acquired his messy habits from his parents. At the end of the hallway, Mom and Dad's room was in total chaos.

Spark noticed Mom's makeup kit splayed out on the dresser, its contents spilled beside a poorly folded stack of laundry. Dad's half-built exercise machine leaned against the wall. The wardrobe doors hung open, and several jackets lay draped over the unmade bed. Mom and Dad never recovered from their early days as parents, and the children were now old enough to notice. "How come I have to clean my room and you don't?" Loretta often asked. Mom always swore she would clean it soon. Dad's typical answer was even more annoying: "When you pay for your own room, then it can be as messy as you want."

Spark also checked the bathroom and the linen closet, but neither yielded clues. She would have to venture downstairs, alone. Something she had never done before. Something Sir Reginald had warned her to never do, to never even *think* about.

Spark lay on the top step, on her tummy. She poked her head through the bars on the railing. A Persian rug covered the living room floor from the fireplace to the front door. Framed photos lined the mantelpiece, arranged from oldest to newest.

Near the edge of the mantel, a trophy towered over the family photos. It was mounted on a marble base, with a golden movie projector at the top. It was the Spirit Award from the Young Filmmakers contest, given to the most popular entry in the competition. Matthew and Loretta won it the year before for their short film, a space-opera parody that earned a standing ovation. Spark allowed herself a smile when she saw it. Even during a crisis, a reminder that her dusa was special always made her a little happier.

The feeling lasted only a few seconds. Through the large archway, Spark could see the breakfast table. And right away, she knew that something was off. Dad was already dressed and ready to go, in a rain slicker and rubber boots and a baseball cap fitted over his graying hair. His sunglasses perched on the brim of the hat, which meant that at some point he would ask where they were. He ate a bowl of cold cereal while leaning against the counter. Matthew zipped his coat, a toasted waffle sticking out of his mouth. Mom ate the last of her banana, dropped the peel in the trash, and buttoned her jacket. In the corner, Loretta struggled to fit her ponytail under her cap.

They were going somewhere, and no one looked happy about it.

The radio on the counter played the news station. The anchor gave the five-day forecast. Unexpectedly mild, with a chance of rain later in the week.

The family ate in near silence. Mom looked like she wanted to say something. Finally, she asked, "Is Darcy going?"

Darcy was Loretta's best friend. "Of course she's going, Mom," Loretta said. "Everyone is."

While the family finished breakfast, Spark scanned the room. Nothing seemed out of place. Across from the kitchen was the den, where the children often watched movies on the flat-screen television. Spark heard a noise coming from that direction. It sounded like a machine whirring. If she could get there without being seen, maybe she would find something useful. Zed's voice whined in her head: *You're not supposed to do that!*

Spark tried to remember her training. In the early days, Sir Reginald used to time her as she zipped from the den to the kitchen to the staircase, all without making a sound. It never seemed fair—the faster she went, the louder her footsteps were. "You will learn," the old bear told her. "You will blend in. And you will be prepared if the day comes."

She readied herself. Dad's snow boots sat on the bottom step, tall enough for Spark to hide behind. She curled into a ball and tumbled, her brown fur whispering against the stairs. She came to rest right behind the boots.

With Dad facing her from the kitchen, Spark waited for him to pour more coffee before she could move again. As the news anchor began the traffic report, Dad turned away from the living room. Spark dashed across the rug and somersaulted into the den, landing on the carpet. It gave off a new smell, like plastic and smoke.

After making sure no one was watching, she climbed to her feet and hopped onto the recliner. Beside it, the family computer sat on the desk, with rows of books on the shelves behind it. A pile of manila folders leaned precariously on the edge.

Spark jumped from the recliner and latched onto the edge of the desk. The printer spat out page after page, building a stack over two inches thick. They were flyers, printed in black and white, each with a photo of a girl in the middle. The printer stopped, either because it had finished the job or because it had run out of paper.

"Lemme have your granola bar," Matthew said in the kitchen.

"I'm not done with it yet," Loretta said.

"You're not gonna eat it."

"Mom."

"Let her eat it," Mom said, annoyed.

The radio switched off. Footsteps approached.

In a panic, Spark swiped the top flyer and folded it under her arm. She immediately regretted it. Being found out of place was bad enough, but getting caught with something important in her paw would probably terrify the entire family, maybe convince them that the house was haunted. But it was too late to put it back. Dad's shadow darkened the doorway. Spark dove between the recliner and the desk, her wide hips wedged between the fabric and the wood. She tried to twist herself free, but this made a rubbing noise. The paper crinkled. Spark froze when Dad's boot pressed down just a few inches away.

"Is it finished printing?" Mom called from the other room.

"Yeah," Dad said. As he lifted the flyers from the printer, he bumped one of the manila folders. It was enough to tip the entire stack over the edge. Spark braced herself. Dad tried to catch them, but the folders plummeted into the space between the chair and the desk. The weight of them squished Spark into an odd shape, with her ears flattened against her head and her legs twisted around her neck.

"What happened?" Mom asked.

"Nothing. I'm fine."

Spark wanted to squirm her way free, but it was best to remain still and hope Dad didn't notice. So stupid to come here—to risk everything like this. Sir Reginald would never have allowed it.

Sir Reginald isn't here, she told herself. No one was coming to the rescue.

"Did something fall?" Mom asked.

"It's nothing. I'll fix it later."

As soon as Dad rejoined the others in the kitchen, Spark worked her way free. She smoothed the creases in her fur. No damage done. No stuffing lost.

"Here, take a few," Dad said. Spark could hear the papers rustling as Dad handed each of them a stack.

She unfolded the flyer and stared at it for a long time. Sir Reginald had taught her how to read, late at night when no one would hear. She traced the words with her paw, whispering them to herself, still unable to believe them.

Outside, the family piled into the SUV. The engine started.

"Come on!" Matthew said.

"I'm right behind you," Loretta said. "OMFG!"

"Watch it with the language," Mom said.

"They're letters, Mom."

"I know what the letters mean."

By the time the vehicle drove away, Spark finally accepted what was right in front of her. She didn't want to. And she had no idea what to do next.

THREE

Clutching the flyer to her chest, Spark dashed up the stairs and into Loretta's room. On the shelf, Zed sat with his legs dangling over the ledge.

"Monkey, get down here," Spark said.

Zed stared at the flyer. "Where did you get that?"

"Never mind where I got it. I need you to see it."

"Sir Reginald said we're not supposed to take things."

Spark shook the folded paper at him. "If I have to climb up there to get you, I swear I'm tossing you out the window. Now come here."

Zed pushed himself off the edge and landed on the floor with a thud.

"You need to see this," Spark said. "I know I'm the protector here, but this is about all of us now. Do you understand?"

"No."

Sighing, Spark unfolded the flyer and smoothed it out on the floor. In the center, a crease ran through the black-and-white image of the girl. It was a school picture. The girl sat in front of a screen and smiled, wearing a basketball jersey over a T-shirt. The team name was the Cardinals, the mascot of Loretta and Matthew's school. She had straight, shiny hair parted in the middle of her head and dangling in two pigtails. The word MISSING splashed across the top of the page. Her personal information appeared beneath the image. Name: Sofia Lopez. Height: 5 feet, 4 inches. Age: 13. Hair color: black. Eyes: brown. Distinguishing characteristics: a surgical scar on her stomach. Zed traced his finger along the contact information, the hotline people could call if they knew anything. CALLS ARE ANONYMOUS, it promised.

And then, the worst part. The part that punched Spark in her gut. In capital letters, a simple, desperate plea: HELP US PLEASE. She heard the phrase in Loretta's voice every time she read it.

"Who's that?" Zed asked.

"She goes to school with Loretta and Matthew."

Loretta and Sofia had played on the same basketball team the year before. While Loretta spent most of the season on the bench, Sofia played center, because she was taller than most of the boys in her class. When Loretta told her about her and Matthew's filmmaking hobby, Sofia offered to help. Her uncle worked for the local news station, and his computer used the same kind of editing software that Mom and Dad had bought Matthew for his birthday. Sofia showed Matthew how to use it, which gave their movies a professional quality. It probably won them the Spirit Award.

And as a result, Matthew developed a huge crush on her.

Sir Reginald told Spark all about it, but she got to witness it firsthand the day Sofia came to the house to teach Matthew the program. The boys at school did not understand Matthew and his unusual interests. Some bullies picked on him so much that Spark once asked if she and Sir Reginald should accompany Matthew to class, to protect him. The old bear told her no. Matthew needed to learn on his own. And despite all that, here Matthew was, inviting the most popular girl in school to his house.

He purposely met with her on a day when Loretta wouldn't be home—he didn't want any interference. He wore his best shirt and khakis and splashed on some cheap cologne that Spark could smell through the walls. Though it took only a few minutes for Sofia to walk him through the software, Matthew tried to make the visit last as long as possible. Sofia was patient enough to let him go on and on about his favorite films. When they both agreed that some of the Marvel superhero movies were overrated, Matthew acted like they jointly discovered some hidden secret of the universe.

As Sofia made her way out of the house, Matthew followed behind like a puppy, trying to slow her exit with more questions. Sofia cut it short with a simple demand: "You better put my name in the credits of all your movies."

"Oh, yeah, of course!" Matthew said.

"Like, at the *top*," Sofia added.

Matthew stammered some more until she punched him in the arm—Spark could hear it. "I'm joking with you!" she said.

"Sort of."

Spark tried to explain all of this to Zed, but the monkey claimed that he didn't remember Sofia. That was probably because he shut his eyes and clamped his ears whenever strangers entered the house.

"So they can't find her?" he asked.

"No. She's missing."

"Well, where did she go?"

"She's *missing*, Zed. That means nobody knows."

There was more. While searching for clues in the den, Spark had tapped the keyboard to make the computer come to life. Dad's email appeared on the monitor, and it opened to a message from someone named Nick. The message started with a time and place where people would meet. According to the details that followed, the parents in the neighborhood had organized an event at which everyone would hand out the flyers and stick them to every telephone pole and brick wall in town. After that, they would help the police search the woods. That explained the hiking clothes the family wore.

Upon hearing this, Zed grabbed a corner of the paper and spun it toward him so that he could look the missing girl in the face.

"They've been searching for Sofia for a week now," Spark said. "I've been so stupid."

That was it. It was her job to watch over this house. And yet she had been so happy that Loretta needed her again that she didn't ask any questions. So when Matthew sulked around the house these last few days, hiding in his room, Spark told herself that he was turning into a typical teenager. When Mom and Dad stayed up late, speaking in hushed voices, she assumed they were talking about parent stuff: a new job maybe, or a visit from relatives, or paying the bills, or whatever. Looking back, Spark was amazed at how easily she had fooled herself. How badly she wanted to believe that things were okay.

"Maybe Sofia ran away," Zed said.

Most monsters liked to scare children, nothing more. They fed on a child's fear. It had been years since a monster had actually *taken* a child. But the creature from last night, with his pincer tail and grasping claws, seemed ready to do just that.

"Sofia did *not* run away!" Spark said, before realizing that she'd raised her voice too loud. "That thing took her," she whispered.

"No!" Zed said. "No, no, no!" He covered his ears.

"The monster took her—"

"Stop! Stop it!"

"—and it's coming for Loretta next. I saw the way it looked at her."

Zed cried so hard that his entire body shook. Such a cowardly thing, not fit for fighting. But Spark needed him. She needed all the help she could get.

"Do you think the monster took Sir Reginald, too?" Zed asked.

"Maybe." It was possible that Sir Reginald had gone snooping around the house in the night, as he was always sensing danger. Now that Matthew no longer played with him, Sir Reginald had more freedom of movement. Spark pictured the old bear latching onto the monster's tail, shouting the oath of the League of Ursus until the Founders themselves could hear him. The creature could have easily dragged the bear into the portal.

"We need Sir Reginald," she said. "We can't do this without him."

"Do what? And what do you mean *we*?"

"We have to scare this monster off somehow. You can help me, or I can use you as bait. Take your pick."

Like a real monkey, Zed pounded his hands on the floor and squeaked a few times. It was supposed to be scary.

"Are you always like this?" he asked. "Are you always about doing your duty, rah-rah, all that?"

"Yes," Spark said.

It was Sir Reginald's fault. He made her like this. She could not help but think of the time he made her recite the oath while balancing on the basement rafters like a gymnast. Or the time he made her chase squirrels off the roof to quicken her reflexes. "A test!" he shouted. "If you cannot chase a squirrel, you cannot chase a monster!"

Zed gazed at Sofia's smiling face. "So now what?"

"I'm going to find Sir Reginald," Spark said. "If the monster wants this house, he'll have to go through both of us."

FOUR

With the family gone, Spark could focus on the most obvious place to look for Sir Reginald: Matthew's room. The last time she snuck in, several years earlier, action figures lined the shelves and images of X-wing fighters flew across the bedsheets. Today, she entered the room of a boy trying to outgrow these things. All the toys were gone, replaced with books that Matthew had divided into a section for novels and a section on filmmaking. A tripod held a camera in the middle of the rug, and a desktop computer sat near the window. Bright yellow Post-it notes stuck out from the sides of the monitor, and a mess of papers overwhelmed everything else on the desk.

Loretta owned a good number of movie posters, but Matthew's room was covered with them from floor to ceiling. His love of movies helped to pass the time, since he spent much of his childhood in and out of the hospital, and in and out of surgery and the physical therapy that always followed. He was born with a genetic condition that made his right arm and right leg much shorter and weaker than the limbs on his left side. Every year or so, the doctors fitted him with a new leg brace or a new crutch.

While he recovered from his second or third surgery, Mom and Dad got him hooked on going to the movies, the only form of entertainment they could afford when they were a young couple. Loretta got into them as well, and as soon as they were able, the kids began stealing Mom's phone to make short movies of their own. The parents eventually bought them a real camera—a combined birthday and Christmas present—mainly to stop the phone theft.

Over time, they got better at making movies. With cardboard, bedsheets, and other household items, they built entire sets in the living room, recreating everything from a *Dungeons & Dragons* maze to the icy planet Hoth from *The Empire Strikes Back*. (It took them an entire weekend to clean up the Styrofoam packing peanuts that they used for snow.)

Those years of practice led to the movie they made for the contest last year. The story was about a group of space pirates tasked with saving the universe. Nothing special about that. But what got the judges' attention was the odd cast of characters. There were no human actors in the movie, only stuffed animals. Spark remembered it well, having "played" one of the lead roles, along with Sir Reginald, of course. This meant staying still while Matthew and Loretta moved them around like puppets. A strange activity, but it beat sitting on the shelf. For the first time in years, she got to play with her dusa, something she began to think would never happen again.

Matthew's room was an even bigger disaster than usual, which meant he was in full filmmaker mode again. Spark stepped over a sock and a T-shirt, ducked under the legs of the tripod, and popped her head inside the closet. A wooden chest fit snugly in the corner. It was here that Sir Reginald would tap on the wall at three in the morning. She called his name. When he didn't answer, she lifted the lid of the chest. Nothing inside but old toys—spaceships, plastic swords, and a pair of walkie-talkies that never worked.

Spark closed the lid, pressed her shoulder against the chest, and slid it a few inches. Underneath, she found a symbol that Sir Reginald had carved into the floorboard many years earlier. It consisted of a circle with two bear paws inside. One paw held a sword and the other held a lightning bolt. If a human were to find the etching—especially an adult—they would dismiss it as an imperfection in the wood. But Spark knew what it meant. It was the symbol of the League, and it warned all monsters to stay away from this house.

And yet the monster she saw last night did not seem to care.

There was another symbol she needed to find. Spark hopped onto the windowsill. She lifted the screen and poked her head outside. Right below the window frame, she expected to see a trio of paw prints in the shape of a triangle, drawn with ink or dirt or soap. It would wash away in the rain, another tiny imperfection that humans would dismiss. The paw prints signaled danger to the other teddy bears in the neighborhood. Not the most effective system of communicating, but it was what they had used for generations. Word would spread through the League, all the way to the high council, and help would arrive. When that would happen, and what form the help would take, Spark could not say.

But the triangle was not there. Sir Reginald must have gone missing before he could paint it. So Spark took a dry-erase marker from a cup full of pens on Matthew's desk and drew it herself. After she finished, she stared at it for a few seconds, hoping it would make her feel safer. Maybe it would later.

She moved on to the desk. The papers scattered about were storyboards—big sheets with six squares drawn on each. Inside each square, Matthew had sketched an image from the movie, a shot they wanted to make. The storyboards were basically a map of an entire film, from beginning to end. One page showed Spark and Sir Reginald scaling the side of a castle with ropes. Another showed them escaping from a burning building—though this one had an X drawn through it. Loretta's handwriting appeared at the top: "Don't need this—too difficult to shoot!!"

Spark tried to piece together the story from the images. Whereas their first big movie was science fiction, this follow-up was definitely a fantasy. As far as she could tell, Spark would play a knight who fought in some great war many years earlier. The king, played by Sir Reginald, was killed in the Battle of the Black Mountains, his body never found. The evil prince replaced him and ruled the land with an iron fist. The contest judges loved that stuff. A deadly serious story acted out by ridiculous stuffed animals would definitely get their attention again.

Spark continued flipping through the pages. Eventually, the hero discovers that the king is still alive and is being held prisoner far away in a dungeon guarded by a dragon. She begins a quest to find him and return him to the throne. Joining the search is a handful of misfits: a mercenary, a magician, and a jester.

Spark moved on to the computer. She nudged the mouse and the monitor came to life. A browser window appeared in the center of the screen. It showed Loretta and Matthew's YouTube channel, which they called *Loretta and Matthew Love Movies!*, or *LM*^{2} for short. Spark knew she had work to do, but she clicked the play button anyway. She needed to see them. She needed to pretend that everything was okay.

The video began. Loretta and Matthew appeared side by side in front of a blank white background. Loretta wore a purple dress, while Matthew wore a tux. That was Matthew's idea—he thought they should look glamorous, like presenters at the Academy Awards. And sure enough, the first commenter, someone named JohnCarpenterFan78, said that they loved the outfits.

"Hi everyone!" Loretta said. "Welcome to Episode 22 of *LM*^{2}! Today we're talking about . . ."

"The power of zoom!" they shouted together. The camera zoomed in for an intense close-up. They both shouted "whoaaa!" as if the camera were attacking them.

"But before we get started," Matthew said, "we would love to have you become an official LM Square." He pointed off-screen. "Click over here to subscribe to our channel."

Every episode had the same setup. Loretta and Matthew would talk about a filmmaking technique and how a director used it in a famous movie. Then they would demonstrate how the technique worked, all in about five minutes. Spark had clicked on their most recent video, posted only a few days before, and it had already racked up over three thousand views.

"Today, we're looking at an old movie, but one you all know about," Loretta said. "If your parents are cool, ask them to show you . . ."

Matthew unrolled one of his posters, revealing the image of a shark rising toward the ocean surface. "*Jaws*!" Matthew shouted.

They both started humming the iconic theme music. "Da-dun. Da-dun. Dun-dun dun-dun dun-dun *dun*-dun dun-dun . . ." Matthew made the sound of a horn out of the side of his mouth.

While clips from the movie played, the pair took turns explaining the plot. "A giant shark terrorizes the town of Amity," Loretta said. "People are getting gobbled up left and right!"

"And three men go on a mission to hunt down the hungry fish," Matthew said, "a police chief, a marine biologist, and a crazy old fisherman."

Spark remembered this movie well. Mom and Dad made the mistake of showing it to the children when they were too young. Afterward, they sat on the edge of Loretta's bed and explained to her that she was safe, that the beach they went to every summer did not have a great white shark swimming around. Before long, Loretta tried watching it again and loved it. From then on, she acted as though she had never been scared of it in the first place.

"Today, we want to focus on this scene in particular," Matthew said. On-screen was Police Chief Brody, the hero of the film, sitting on a beach chair with his wife, Ellen, behind him. He stared out past the camera, into the ocean.

"This is the big moment, when he sees the shark grab a kid in the water!" Matthew said.

The camera zoomed in on Brody's face so fast that it warped the space around him, creating a dizzying effect, like staring down from the top of a skyscraper.

"This is the classic dolly zoom," Loretta said. "You put the camera on wheels, shove it really fast at your actor, and the background kind of falls away."

They used a crude diagram, drawn on printer paper, showing the camera on one side, a stick figure on the other, and a pair of diagonal lines to show the camera's range.

"We feel the character's emotions as they come face-to-face with the thing they fear the most," Loretta said. "They can't run away from it! They can only move forward!"

Spark remembered Loretta squeezing her for comfort the first time she watched this scene. She skipped ahead in the video to when Loretta and Matthew attempted to recreate the zoom shot using a rolling chair as a dolly.

"Okay, so let's say this is a monster," Matthew said, dropping Sir Reginald on his bed. "And I'm Chief Brody, I guess. Loretta will be shooting."

A quick shot of Sir Reginald as the "monster," though he was little more than a ball of black fur.

The camera zeroed in on Matthew. His eyes widened and his jaw dropped as he pretended to see the shark. The "dolly" rolled toward him on squeaky wheels.

"Oh, crap," Loretta said. The camera jostled right before the lens bonked Matthew square on the nose, leaving a giant smudge in the middle of the screen.

Matthew covered his face with his hand. "Loretta!"

"Sorry," she said off-screen. "I slipped!" A little hitch sound in her throat let Spark know that she was trying not to laugh.

Matthew glared at her, though he came close to laughing as well.

"Can we leave that in the video?" Loretta asked.

"You . . . you did that on purpose!"

"What? No!"

He waited. And soon, Loretta couldn't hold it in any longer. The camera shook as she fell into a fit of giggles.

"Okay, cut," Matthew said.

"You have a greasy nose," Loretta said.

"Shut up. Take two."

Spark giggled along with them as they set up the shot again. But then she shook it off. She had a job to do. With the video still running, she clicked on the window and moved it aside. Another window hid behind it, this one open to an article from the local newspaper. In big black letters, the headline read, SEARCH FOR MISSING GIRL REACHES FOURTH DAY. As Spark scrolled the page, the same black-and-white image of Sofia Lopez from the flyer climbed upward, like a ghost rising from the earth. Spark froze stiff when she saw it. Beneath the image, the article talked about the community coming together to try to find her. Matthew must have read the article that very morning.

Matthew's crush on Sofia was part of growing up, Sir Reginald often said. Spark hoped that the boy would have the courage to tell her someday, after this was all over, and to be okay with whatever happened after that.

While Sofia stared out from the screen, the video continued to play. "That's how you do a dolly zoom!" Loretta said.

"Just try not to crash into things," Matthew said. "Or people!"

The video ended with the brother and sister asking the audience to give it a try themselves. And then they said their catchphrase together: "Keep dreaming, and keep trying!"

Spark moved the window over the image of Sofia again. This was what she was fighting for. Every bear had a special dusa, the most wonderful child in the whole world. And so did she.

She slid off the chair. There were more places to search, and she was running out of time.

FIVE

Spark tried the attic next. With the door locked, she could only pound on it and call Sir Reginald's name. He didn't answer.

On to the basement, where Dad kept his tools and workbench, and Mom her softball equipment. Loretta used to bring Spark here, but with the musty smell, exposed pipes, and spiderwebs in the rafters, she never stayed long. It was a quiet, mostly forgotten part of the house. Once again, Sir Reginald failed to respond when she called for him.

Spark checked the closets, under the furniture, behind the shelves. Nothing.

She looked out the window, at the neighbor's house. A boy named Jared lived there, much younger than Matthew and Loretta. Jared made no secret that he wanted to own Sir Reginald. He saw the bear in Matthew's window one day and fell in love with him. More than once, he even rang the doorbell and asked if Sir Reginald could come out and play. Matthew resented it at first, but Mom told him that Jared meant no harm, and that the boy had been lonely ever since his father died.

But no. If Matthew planned to give him away, Sir Reginald would have warned her. He would have said goodbye. Something must have happened, something neither of them saw coming.

That left the garage as the last place to search. Sir Reginald had left something there for Spark, in case they ever got separated during an attack.

Spark went to the window in the kitchen that faced the backyard, where the green grass was slowly beginning to replace the brown—a welcome sign of spring. Beyond that, the garage waited. It was a small structure with peeling white paint and dust-caked windows. From here, the building seemed like miles away. This was too much. Spark had already tempted fate by prowling around the house. But leaving the house entirely, and risking getting caught in the open, would put teddy bears everywhere in danger. Who was she to make such a choice?

Spark asked herself this question as she climbed onto a chair and turned the doorknob. She asked it again as she placed her foot on the wooden deck, another forbidden country she never imagined conquering alone. The question continued to rattle in her head—in Sir Reginald's voice, of course—as she descended the staircase and landed on the grass. And still, her mind could not figure out the answer. She wanted to find her friend. She wanted to protect her dusa. Those reasons would have to be enough.

The grass tickled her ankles and legs. The leaves were colder than she expected. She glanced behind at the tracks she had made. Too many clues. She needed to move quickly, get out of sight before anyone noticed.

The garage door had an electronic mechanism to open it. But long ago Sir Reginald showed her that the door could rise a few inches if she put her weight into it. Lifting the handle was easier this time, and Spark managed to roll underneath before the door dropped to the ground again.

Once inside, she found the place even more cluttered than she remembered. Sir Reginald told her that the garage was for the car, and yet the family had stored so much junk here over the years that the vehicle would no longer fit. Four bicycles—two for adults, two for children—leaned against one wall, next to a weed whacker, a lawnmower, and a stack of dusty plastic chairs. Clay pots rose in a column that almost reached the ceiling. With all this stuff, the space in the middle of the concrete floor had shrunk to the size of a tabletop.

Amid the clutter, there remained a tiny crevice between a metal cabinet and the wall. A fine crack in the floor showed the wear and tear on the concrete. Or so the humans were supposed to believe. When Spark got on all fours and pressed her paw beside the crack, a piece of the concrete came loose, lifting away from the foundation. Sir Reginald had deemed this the best place to hide something.

Part of Spark wanted to find it. Part of her didn't.

When she tilted the slab away, she found a shiny piece of metal—a tiny, double-edged sword, only a few inches long. The perfect length for a teddy bear with stubby arms. Not big enough to fight a monster, though certainly big enough to make an intruder think twice about getting close. To drive that point home, the blacksmith who forged the sword inscribed the word *protector* on every inch of the blade, in all the languages the bears used in the early days of the League. Latin. Arabic. Mandarin. Old English. A tight leather strap wrapped around the handle, giving it a nice grip, and on the base of the blade was the symbol of the League. The metal hissed as she pulled it from its resting place.

This was Sir Reginald's sword. The high council of the League gave it to him as a reward for chasing off a monster many years ago. He called it Arctos, taken from *Ursus arctos horribilis*, the scientific name for the grizzly bear. He placed the sword here not only to keep it safe, but also because he thought he might never need to use it again, since most of the monsters were driven into hiding long ago.

On her knees, Spark gripped the sword in both paws, with its point on the ground. She leaned on the handle and tried to think of what to do next. But her mind kept drifting to the past, because on this very spot, years earlier, Sir Reginald first told her about the League and their sacred mission.

It was not long after Mom and Dad gave her to Loretta as a present. Back then, Loretta was a tiny baby with barely any hair, while Spark was merely a clump of cloth and fake brown fur, with two marbles for eyes. Once the girl met her, Spark came to life. She woke up, as the bears liked to call it. Everything she knew was Loretta. Every word she could speak was about watching over the child, staying as close as possible— though Spark did not yet have a name. (It would be a few years before Mom taught Loretta that a spark was a tiny bright particle shooting from an open flame, or a flash from an electrical current. Or it could mean something burning inside someone—a sense of bravery, a taste for adventure. Once Mom put it that way, Loretta knew what to call her bear. Afterward, it felt like Spark had known her name all along.)

Lucky for her, the old bear sought her out in those early days. As soon as Mom and Dad took Loretta to Grandma's for the first time, he appeared in the girl's room and introduced himself as Sir Reginald the Brave. He repeated the Founders' code, the one all the bears knew by heart: "Bears serve. Bears watch. Bears protect. Always and forever."

Somehow, Spark knew right away what it meant.

"Come on, little cub," he said. "There is much you need to learn."

It was the beginning of her training. He showed her all the closets and windows, the dark corners and the open spaces. All the hiding places. Finally, he took her to the backyard, which seemed so wide open that Spark felt she could fall into it and drift far away in the wind. Sir Reginald told her that a lot of newly awakened bears found the outdoors too frightening. Spark took this as a challenge, which it was, so she marched boldly across the lawn with him.

As soon as they entered the garage, Sir Reginald vanished. "Where'd you go?" Spark asked, starting to panic.

"A test!" his voice said. It seemed to come from everywhere. "There will be surprises! You must think fast if you want to be a good bear!"

She noticed movement overhead; a plastic flowerpot, hanging from the rafters by a hook, swung back and forth ever so slightly. And it was the perfect size to conceal a bear. She climbed the shelves. Once on top, she reached for the flowerpot and tried to tip it over, giggling a little. At that exact moment,

Sir Reginald popped out from behind a toolbox. He startled her so completely that she lost her footing and plummeted to the floor. He jumped and landed beside her.

"This is no game, young hotshot!" he said. "You must be ready!"

"For what?"

"Anything! But mostly monsters."

"Monsters?" she asked.

"Bears scare the monsters away. That's what the League is for."

"What league?"

"The League of Ursus," he said. "Bears that keep watch."

That was when he showed her the sword.

"It is an honor to be recruited into the League," he said. "I have never heard of a bear saying no."

"How do you know I'll be any good at this?" Spark asked.

"I was once Dad's bear," he said. "He was once my dusa. When he grew into a man, with a family of his own, he passed me on to Matthew."

At only a few weeks old, Spark could hardly imagine time stretching back that far.

"I have been watching over this family for two generations," Sir Reginald said. "And I can see that you love your dusa as much as any bear could. That is all that matters."

He asked her to kneel. Then he tapped the flat part of the sword on each of her shoulders and once between her ears. "May you protect your dusa through all her days, bright or dark."

"I don't even have a name yet," she said.

"You will. Maybe someday you'll earn a sword, too."

Back in the present, Spark gripped the handle of Arctos. She needed to get back to the house. Rising to her feet, she tucked the sword under her arm and crawled under the garage door.

On her way across the lawn, Spark gazed at the roof, hoping that Sir Reginald would stick his fuzzy black ears over the side. But she saw nothing.

"Three at three tonight," she said to herself. "Three at—"

She stopped dead when a furry creature blocked her path. It was a squirrel, so skinny from his long winter's sleep that he looked like a wool sock, his tail thicker than his body. Not one of the squirrels she had chased as part of her training, but maybe a descendant. He rose onto his hind legs and stared at her with his dark, wet eyes.

Spark did not have time for this. She waved the sword and growled. The squirrel bounded away, his tail a fluffy blur as he raced across the yard. Maybe the monster would do the same thing, once he realized that this house was under the protection of the League.

On her way to the bedroom, Spark decided to hide the sword from Zed. He would have too many questions, and she had no time to answer them. So she lifted the rug in the hallway, right by the closet with the cleaning supplies, and slipped it underneath.

As she patted the rug into place, the family car rolled into the driveway. With slamming doors and stomping footsteps, the family entered the house, moving faster than she expected. Spark left the sword behind and hurried to her spot on the shelf.

SIX

Loretta walked right past Spark, went straight to her laptop, and started searching for information related to Sofia. She clicked through the local news sites, along with some kind of chatroom in which people posted the latest rumors. To help her focus, Loretta put on giant headphones and listened to her music at a deafening volume.

Zed tapped his foot on the shelf above Spark. "*Pssst*," he said, "You were on the bed when she left this morning. Not the shelf."

He was right. But with so many other things on her mind, Loretta hadn't noticed.

"Well, you're not supposed to talk when she's in the room," Spark said.

"Neither are you!"

"You're still talking."

His tail batted the shelf in anger. "No, you're . . . because you . . ."

She could barely contain her laughter. "Shut *up*, Zed."

And so he did.

Sometime later, Loretta closed her laptop and left the room. Spark followed the sound of her footsteps to Matthew's door. Loretta knocked, and Matthew opened. Spark dropped from her perch and raced to the closet. Zed let out a little yip in protest. Once inside, Spark pressed her ear to the wall and listened. She imagined Matthew at his desk, elbows on the armrests of his chair, while Loretta sat on the bed with her legs crossed.

"Well, lemme see," Loretta said.

Some papers rustled as Matthew showed her the latest storyboards.

"Where are we gonna get one of these?" Loretta said. She asked this about the props or scenery in almost every storyboard Matthew drew.

"Mr. Apelian is letting me borrow one from his shop class," Matthew said.

"Okay, but, here's the thing . . ." Whenever Loretta wanted to say something without really saying it, she started like this. "There's that other contest you told me about in the fall, and that's an even bigger deal, right? So what if we, like, ya know, worked on the script a little more—"

"The script is fine," Matthew said.

"It's just—Jisha said she might not be able to help us now, because her parents have been really strict since, you know . . ."

She trailed off.

"You don't want to do the movie," Matthew said.

"No, I do! But, this thing that's going on . . ."

Spark imagined Loretta waving her arms about.

"You know what I mean," she said.

"You mean with Sofia?"

"Yes, I mean with Sofia!"

A long pause. "Mom said the same thing," Matthew said. Loretta exhaled.

"But we're doing it anyway," he added.

"Come on—"

"You heard all the parents talking about Sofia at the search, didn't you?"

"Yeah."

"They're wrong. Okay? Sofia didn't run away. I know she hates her dad sometimes, but she didn't run away."

"So what happened to her?"

Matthew sighed. "Look, this is gonna sound crazy. I'm just telling you what she told me."

"Okay."

"She's a superstitious person. She believes in magic and parallel universes and stuff like that."

"I know that," Loretta said. "She had a bracelet she wore on the basketball team. She said it helped her make jump shots."

"Right. Well, there were some other things she believed in. A few days before she disappeared, she told me about some weird stuff going on at her house."

Loretta paused. "What kind of weird stuff?"

"She, uh . . ." Matthew paused. Spark imagined him scratching the back of his neck, which he often did when he was embarrassed. "When she was a kid, she thought there was a monster under her bed. Last week she told me that she saw it again. And then, just a couple days later . . . she vanished."

Loretta did not respond. In the dead space, Spark knew that she was thinking of her own run-in with a monster the night before. She had probably tried to dismiss it as a bad dream. Spark could imagine Loretta's mind processing all of this, a tiny voice in her head shouting *No no no* until she could compose herself.

"All I know is that she was a little freaked out," Matthew said. "Almost like she knew something bad was gonna happen."

"What's that got to do with finishing the movie?"

"Sofia made me promise that we would finish it no matter what. And she's the one who convinced me to change the ending."

"She told you to add all that magic stuff?"

"Yeah."

"I knew it!" Loretta gasped. "You were acting so weird about it. I knew it must have been her!"

"Just listen to me, okay?" Matthew said. "She thinks—and I know this is weird—but she thinks that what we're doing, all this, is a good thing. There's all this bad stuff in the world, so we're doing good stuff. To . . . fight it, or whatever."

Before today, it would have sounded silly to Spark.

"Oh my God," Loretta said. "You really *do* have a crush on her!"

"Shut up!"

"Is the movie, like, casting a spell or something?" She laughed.

"I don't believe this stuff either, I'm just telling you what she said!"

Spark could tell from his tone that this was not entirely true. Matthew was at least open to what Sofia had told him.

"I promised her I would finish it," he said. "What are we supposed to do? Stop everything?"

"I don't know," Loretta said. "Maybe it wouldn't be cool to keep going without her."

"But she would want us to!" Matthew said. "Look, her dad told her that all this movie stuff was a waste of time."

"So?"

"So that's why Sofia told me that she's jealous of us. Jealous that we get to do stuff like this. That we can create things—not for school, just for fun—and we don't have to hide it."

Oh, that's huge, Spark thought. Loretta admired Sofia. Everyone did. Maybe Matthew knew that, and knew exactly what Loretta needed to hear.

"But the same goes for you," Matthew said. "If I wasn't here, you would finish the movie without me. Because we've worked too hard. Right?"

"Well—"

"Don't *well* me! This is important! The deadline's coming up!"

"All right, all right," she said. "I would finish the movie without you. Okay? I'd make it better."

"You can try!" Spark heard Matthew's chair swivel away from her, toward his computer.

"If you're sure, then let's film it this week," Loretta said.

"I'll tell Darcy and the others."

Loretta's feet padded all the way to the door, where they stopped. "Matthew."

He swiveled toward her again. "Yeah?"

"Are you okay?"

"I'm fine."

"I mean, I get that you wanna do the movie still, but . . . are you okay? It's okay to be worried about her. I'm worried too."

Spark pressed her ear even closer to the wall. She heard a choking sound. And then Loretta ran over to Matthew, and the two of them sniffled together for a few seconds.

"Shut the door," Matthew said. "Shut the door! Shut it!" She ran to the door, slammed it, and returned to Matthew, where the two of them hugged and cried for nearly a minute. Lately Matthew had been trying to hide his emotions, to act tough, but no one could keep that up forever.

"They're looking in the wrong places," Matthew said. "I want to do something. I want to find her myself. I *know* she didn't run away."

"I know. It's going to be okay. They'll find her. Or she'll come back. Maybe we can investigate on our own tomorrow or something."

"Yeah, maybe. Don't tell Mom I was . . . you know."

"I won't."

Amid the muffled noises of their sobbing, Spark left the closet and climbed to her spot on the shelf.

"Did you hear anything?" Zed whispered.

"They're fine," Spark replied. "Just revising the script."

A few minutes later, Loretta entered her room, wiping tears from her face. She blew her nose into a tissue and then lay on her bed for a little bit, thinking.

Spark watched until Loretta got up and went downstairs to the kitchen, probably for a snack. Before long, night would fall once more. Spark needed to be ready this time.

SEVEN

Despite everything, a single, hopeful phrase stuck in Spark's head: *I'll tell Darcy and the others.* If they were filming the sequel to their big movie, then Spark would see some of her old friends again—the other toys who "acted" alongside her. Maybe they would have advice on how to scare this monster away. If nothing else, they would at least make her feel safer.

Spark could hardly believe that a year had passed since Matthew burst into Loretta's room and announced, "We need actors! Good ones!" Along with Darcy, he had asked Loretta to call her friends Jisha and Claire. "I asked them at your birthday party if they still had their old stuffed animals, and they said yes."

"Why don't you ask the kids in *your* class?" Loretta said.

"I did. Miss Kitzman let me make an announcement during homeroom."

"And?"

"Hunter and Eli said yes. But then . . ." Matthew pinched the bridge of his nose as he recalled the incident. "But then

Christian made fun of them for it, so they backed out."

Loretta sank in her chair.

Like always, Matthew tried to lighten the mood with a joke. "Help me, Loretta," he said like Princess Leia. "You're my only hope."

Whenever her brother got like this, Loretta could never turn him down.

Though Darcy and Jisha said yes right away, it took Loretta two days of begging to get Claire on board. Claire excelled at everything she did. She rode horses and took ballet and won first place two years in a row in a rock-climbing competition. She was busy all the time and always let people know it. So when Loretta asked if they could use her Rana, Amazon Princess™ doll for the movie, Claire offered to simply give it to her. Loretta told her that they needed a voice actor to play the part as well. "It'll be fun," she said. "We're doing a sleepover."

The Rana doll was important because her brand of toys had been around for decades, and Matthew hoped that it would remind the judges of when they were young. Plus, this Rana model was an older version—a classic. Her sword was made of real metal instead of spray-painted plastic. The toy company had to stop selling them because the sword was too sharp, which made this Rana a collector's item.

Claire agreed to help on one condition: that Loretta never tell anyone. She didn't even want her name in the credits. "No offense, but I don't want Khaled to find out what we're doing," she said. Khaled may or may not have had a crush on Claire, according to the many gossip-filled phone conversations Spark overheard.

In addition to wrangling the cast, Loretta insisted on heavily editing Matthew's script. Upon reading it, she immediately declared his teddy bear space opera "a mess." Plus, they needed a strict shooting schedule. They needed to wrap it up before everyone fell asleep, which would happen fast once the s'mores came out. "If we're gonna do it, let's do it right!" she said.

That's the kind of person Loretta was. She was the popular one, the one with all the friends. And she used that power to protect Matthew, when so many other people would have used it for themselves. That was why Spark loved her—not simply because they belonged to one another, but because Loretta was special.

And so they had their cast and a shooting script. Yet they had neglected one thing: getting permission from their parents. Mom and Dad pushed back a little when Matthew suggested filming in the house. "The last time you made a movie in the den, it took a week to clean it up," Dad said. The children assured the parents that nothing would get broken, and they would clean everything up after they were finished.

And then, of course, Matthew went overboard, exactly as Mom and Dad predicted. He spent a week building a movie set in the den that soon intruded on the living room. The parents tolerated it, though Dad complained about not being able to watch basketball.

"The flat-screen is the monitor for the starship," Matthew explained.

"The starship, sure," Dad replied.

On the night of the shoot, Darcy brought Ozzie the polar bear, whose furry white head poked out the top of the girl's backpack. When they were younger, Darcy used to bring him over all the time, but that night was the first time Spark had seen him in years. Jisha carried a panda named Lulu. Both girls swore they had to dig the bears out of storage. Both were lying—Spark confirmed that with Ozzie and Lulu later.

Claire arrived late. Unlike the other girls, who wore hoodies and sweatpants, Claire wore Uggs and lip gloss. At the time, she was the only one among them who owned a cell phone. Impatiently, she pulled Rana, Amazon Princess™ by her slim leg from the bottom of her purse.

Spark had never met one of Rana's kind, and she found the Amazon fascinating. Rana had long tanned legs, leather sandals, a royal-blue cape, and a crown on top of her flowing blonde hair. Compared to the doughy bears, Rana looked like a real warrior. Beautiful and sleek and strong.

Matthew used to have a couple action figures, but he never bonded with them, and so they never came to life like the bears did. Sir Reginald was grateful for that, for he never trusted them. "Made in a factory," he often said. "Toys, nothing more." Of course, Sir Reginald did not even know if he or Spark were made in a factory. They could remember nothing from before their dusa chose them. But it didn't matter. "It is different for us bears," he insisted. "We understand humans. They understand us."

Claire handed Rana over to Loretta and then immediately began texting on her phone. "Sorry," she said, though she was clearly not sorry. Jisha and Darcy looked at each other and rolled their eyes.

The shoot carried on as planned. Loretta kept Matthew on schedule, reminding him that each scene could take only a certain amount of time—otherwise, the entire movie would fall behind and never get finished. Spark remembered being placed in poses. In some scenes, she would battle Sir Reginald or Ozzie. In others, she would stare at an imaginary horizon with her binoculars, or pilot a fighter ship.

Matthew insisted that the space scenes look deliberately fake. He *wanted* it to look like they shot the movie in a living room. That way, it would resemble a child's game of make-believe. "That's what movies are," he said. To achieve the effect, he used a black curtain as a backdrop, with lamplight blazing through tiny holes cut in the cloth. He then dangled the toy spaceships in front of it with fishing wire, like filmmakers did on movie sets fifty years ago.

But Spark barely remembered any of that. It made little sense to her anyway. No, she remembered what happened later, after the movie set closed for the night and the girls dozed off in their sleeping bags on the floor of the den. The other bears, along with Rana, gathered in the corner, sharing their stories in the glow of the nightlight, like a campfire. This almost never happened. So often, toys like them lived solitary lives, rarely interacting with others of their kind. But Loretta and Matthew had brought them all together.

"We are very lucky to be here," Sir Reginald said, so proud of his dusa.

"Yes," Ozzie said. He was a large bear, almost the size of a toddler. He remained well preserved, though a few rough patches on his arm gave away his age. Despite playing the villain in the movie, Ozzie was a gentle giant. Like most bears, he had adopted the traits of his dusa. Taking after Darcy, he was kind, loyal, and honest. More than once, he checked on Darcy to make sure she slept on her side.

"The doctor told her it's better for her back," he said. "She has scoliosis." When Darcy flipped onto her stomach, Ozzie crept over to her and gently batted her cheek until she stirred and rolled into a more comfortable position.

Sir Reginald sometimes spoke poorly of Ozzie, dismissing him as soft, lacking in discipline. Spark used to wonder what life would be like if she were paired with this sweet polar bear instead. Things would be quieter, more fun perhaps. But she would also be less prepared. Less battle ready in the event of an attack.

Lulu, the stout little panda, was mischievous. She enjoyed telling stories of sneaking around the house in broad daylight, eavesdropping on Jisha's mom, moving things out of place as a practical joke. She told the group about a time when Jisha got in trouble for something she didn't do, and her mom confiscated her allowance for the week. Lulu knew how to pick locks, so she broke into the parents' room and retrieved the money.

"You shoulda seen me!" she said, doubling over with laughter. "I'm tellin' ya, I was a cat burglar. No, wait—a *panda* burglar!"

Spark glanced at Sir Reginald, who no doubt disapproved of Lulu's adventures. But even he chuckled. He was probably thinking of how difficult it would have been to train this panda.

"Have things started to change for you?" Ozzie asked. Everyone knew what he meant.

"Yes," Sir Reginald said. "As they get older, we have to watch them from farther and farther away."

"But not *too* far away," Spark said.

Whenever Spark asked why Loretta didn't play with her anymore, Sir Reginald always said the same thing, which he repeated again for them: "Things may change. Things may move on. But still we keep watch."

"I miss the old days," Ozzie said. "I used to be more important to Darcy than almost anything. But I know it couldn't stay like that forever."

"Part of the job," Sir Reginald said.

Spark expected him to launch into one of his speeches about the League of Ursus, and how the Founders endured so much worse than being left on a shelf or in a box. He talked like that whenever Spark asked him what they would do if Matthew ever gave him away to Jared. "I've been given away before," he would say. "I go where I am needed."

"What *is* your job exactly?" Rana asked.

Spark could sense that all the bears wanted to speak. Out of respect for Sir Reginald's age, they let him answer.

"The same as it has been since children first shaped us out of mud and clay," he said. "Since they first carved us from rock. Since they first sewed us together from cloth and wool."

He allowed the silence to settle.

"Well?" Rana asked.

Sir Reginald repeated the Founders' code. "Bears serve. Bears watch. Bears protect. Always and forever." Ozzie and

Lulu whispered it along with him, out of habit.

"But you're not real bears," Rana said. "You're *teddy* bears."

"We were not always called *teddy* bears." Sir Reginald may not have liked the term, but even he had to admit that the invention of teddies brought more of his kind into the world than ever before. Though children had played with toy animals for as long as anyone could remember, bears proved to be the best at scaring off monsters.

"Morris Michtom understood our power," Sir Reginald said. "So did Richard Steiff."

"Who?"

Sir Reginald explained that Michtom invented the teddy bear in New York in 1902. That year, President Theodore "Teddy" Roosevelt had gone hunting for bears in Mississippi. When he couldn't find one, his hunting party captured a cub for him, tied it to a tree, and told Roosevelt to shoot it. Being a good sportsman, the President refused, and after word of the incident spread, Michtom designed his bear toys and named them teddy bears in honor of Roosevelt. Around the same time, Steiff created a similar line of bears in Germany. People still argue over who came up with the idea first. But thanks to their efforts, the teddies soon appeared everywhere, in such great numbers that they forced the monsters into hiding. For more than one hundred years, the monsters mostly stayed away—some hiding in swamps and sewers, the rest living in a world far beyond this one. The ones that stole children mostly died out. The monsters that remained did not kidnap humans. Instead, they fed on children's fear, and their numbers dwindled as well.

"I guess we owe this League of yours a debt of gratitude," Rana said.

"We do not ask for thanks," Sir Reginald said. "Children can see monsters. Most adults cannot. It is our duty to stand by the young ones when no one else can."

"But look at you. You can't fight."

"We rarely have to. Our mere presence is enough to drive the monsters away." Sir Reginald balled his little paw into something resembling a fist. "But make no mistake," he said. "We can fight, if it comes to it."

"Yes, well . . ." Rana brushed her loose hair over her shoulder. "Claire doesn't see monsters anymore. Ever since I killed one. No more fear of the dark for her."

The bears all leaned forward at once. Like Claire, this Rana was cool and poised. Spark hoped that one day, she could be so calm in the face of danger.

"You killed a monster?" she asked.

Rana held her sword high. "It helps to have one of these. And to know how to use it." Spark could not tell if the princess was making fun of her or merely stating a fact.

Spark, Lulu, and Ozzie each admitted that they had never seen a monster. Though they had heard plenty of stories.

"I have seen one," Sir Reginald said. "Long ago, when I was Dad's bear."

Spark knew the story well.

"Did you fight it?" Lulu asked.

"It ran away. They always do."

"Hmmph," Rana mumbled. "No one really knows what they're made of until they actually *fight* a monster."

Ozzie shifted in his seat. Lulu scratched her chin.

Sir Reginald was unfazed. "What did your monster look like?"

"It was dark," Rana said. "I was swinging blindly. What did *yours* look like?"

The bears turned to him.

"Legs like a spider," he said. "One eye on its face, with a mouth like a bear trap. Tentacles that reached out like great big snakes."

"Ooh, did it have wings, too?" Rana asked.

"No wings."

Sir Reginald told her about the high council bestowing the sword Arctos upon him, as a reward. The other bears listened like children hearing about Santa Claus. "I stood before the Grand Sleuth itself!" he declared.

Rana laughed so hard that she snorted. "The grand what?"

"Sleuth. It is the name we use for a group of bears. Like a school of fish. Or a pride of lions."

"A murder of crows," Lulu said. "That one's pretty cool."

"The Grand Sleuth is the high council of the League," Sir Reginald added. "The very bravest bears."

"Where are they?" Rana asked. "Can you give them a call on Claire's cell phone?"

"They never stay in one place for long," he said. "They go where they are needed most. And you do not call them. They call you."

"A congregation of alligators," Lulu said, mostly to herself. "A shrewdness of apes."

"Whatever," Rana said. "We'll all be stored in an attic any day now. Then we just go to sleep and don't wake up. That's what happens to us when the children don't need us anymore."

"You're wrong," Spark said.

She realized too late that she had raised her voice.

"The bravest bears are called to serve on the Grand Sleuth," Spark said. "They offered the honor to Sir Reginald, but he turned it down so he could stay with this family. Isn't that right?"

"It is," Sir Reginald said.

Chuckling, Rana walked over to Spark. "So that's what you've been told. Well, then. No wonder you bears are so committed."

Darcy stirred in her sleep and coughed. Outside, the sky began to shift from black to purple. Soon, Mom's coffee machine would drip, and the neighbor's truck would roll out of the driveway.

"This has been enjoyable," Sir Reginald said. "A good day to meet new friends, fellow protectors. But we may have to call it a night."

"Wait," Spark said, turning to Rana. "How do you kill a monster?"

Rana smiled. "I thought the League of Teddy Bears taught you how to do that."

"It's the League of *Ursus*," Ozzie said. "We were taught, it's true. We just want to hear from a fellow warrior." Ozzie was sincere—not a hint of sarcasm in his voice. Beside him, Lulu leaned in.

Rana rose from her seat and eyed Claire's purse, where she would have to return before the girl awakened. "To be honest with you, little bear, either you can or you can't. There's no teaching it." The Amazon sheathed her sword. So much confidence. Not even Sir Reginald spoke like that, and he knew everything.

Quietly, they broke their little camp and returned to their spots on the floor. Rather than lie on her side, Spark sat upright for a while, waiting for the sun to rise.

EIGHT

As night fell, an eerie calm descended on the house. It was Saturday night. Mom and Dad watched a movie in the den. Matthew worked on the storyboards a little more—though at some point, he must have grown bored and decided to play a video game, a first-person shooter. He got so enmeshed in the action that he accidentally pulled the headphones out of the jack, and the room filled with the sound of shouting and gunfire until he could fix it. Meanwhile, Loretta barely noticed. She lay on her bed reading *Walk Two Moons*, a novel she had picked from a list of books in her English class.

Spark remained on her perch, convincing herself that everything would be fine. Matthew and Loretta would soldier on. Sofia would return on her own. Sir Reginald would tap on the wall at three. Maybe his disappearance was another one of his tests! To see if she could handle things on her own.

"A test," she mumbled. It sounded true.

The noises throughout the house slowly died out for the night. Mom and Dad switched off the television. Matthew slumped in his bed. Knowing that Loretta could hear, he let out a long fart that he must have been holding in for a while. He started giggling halfway through.

Loretta rolled her eyes. "So immature," she said. She set aside her book, switched off the light, and went to sleep.

Spark watched the clock radio. The bright red numbers said 11:53 p.m. In a few hours, she would tap the closet wall, and Sir Reginald would tap back, and everything would be okay.

Loretta flipped over a few times. At one point, she rested on her stomach with her arm slung over the edge of the mattress, snoring so loudly that she woke herself. She rolled again, this time twisting the covers around her legs and sleeping on her side.

Later, something fell in Matthew's room. A hard knock on the floor, with the carpet barely cushioning it. Spark checked the time: 2:51 a.m. After making sure that Loretta was still asleep, she jumped from the shelf and crept into the closet. Once inside, she grabbed a quarter from the jar of coins. She waited. The red numbers on the clock radio continued to tick upward, though the more she checked the time, the slower it seemed to move.

"Come on, Sir Reginald," she said.

At three o'clock exactly, she tapped the wall three times.

Nothing.

To be sure, she got ready to tap it again. And then, barely louder than a mouse, three little knocks sounded from the other side.

All the tension drained from her. She fell to the wall, arms spread, as if she could hug the entire house for returning Sir

Reginald. There was nothing to worry about. He had simply gone on one of his missions around the house, to make sure everything was safe. In the morning, she would hear all about it. They would figure out what to do about the monster then.

Relieved, feeling lighter, she headed for the closet door. And as soon as she reached the threshold, an invisible force swung the door shut, knocking her onto her back and sealing her in the closet. The quarter rolled away and then spun until it stopped.

In this tiny space, now pitch black, the scent of rust and grease overpowered her. She could taste it. Spark knew then that some kind of dark magic had locked her in here. The scratching sound began, followed by a distant, howling wind that tickled her ears. She steadied herself, waiting for the bright orange portal to open in the closet wall.

And then it didn't.

And then she realized that the portal must have opened on the other side.

In Matthew's room.

"No," she said. She grabbed the quarter and tapped it five times. No response. She tapped again. "Come on, come on!"

Something thudded against the wall. She heard a voice, muffled.

"Sir Reginald!" she shouted, no longer caring if her dusa could hear.

Something tapped back. Not a coin this time. Not metal at all. It struck the wall again. Then a third time.

Three at three, she told herself. *Three meant everything was safe.*

Another tap. Then another. Five taps. *Danger.*

She responded with five more of her own. Whatever stood on the other side began knocking on the wall rapidly, like a woodpecker. *Tet-tet-tet-tet-tet-tet-tet.* Then another tapping to her right, another to her left. Spark realized in a moment of cold horror that she was hearing the monster's claws, skittering about like spiders. They scraped along the wall and pulled away just above the floor.

Matthew screamed. Spark spun on her heels and pounded on the door, while the noise in Matthew's room grew deafening, as if a platoon of soldiers stomped on the floors, the walls, and the ceilings all at once. Loretta could not hear. Neither could Mom and Dad. The monster must have cast a spell on the humans—Spark had heard of this kind of power, but never believed it was real.

Matthew screamed again, only this time his voice came from above. The creature had lifted him somehow. The vibrations moved up the wall to the ceiling. Sir Reginald's voice suddenly cut through the clatter and the screaming.

"I command you to be gone!" he said. "In the name of the League of Ursus, I command you—"

A loud whoosh shook the ceiling. The lightbulb hanging in Loretta's closet jiggled on its wire. The noise stopped. Everything had been sucked upward and vanished, leaving nothing but silence.

The closet door clicked open.

Spark tapped the wall five times. There was no response.

NINE

Loretta spent most of the next morning lounging around her room, killing time as the sun climbed higher in the sky. She started her math homework, then checked the stats on the *Jaws* video. A few thousand more views in the night. For the first time since Sofia disappeared, Loretta seemed wide awake, ready to take on a new day. She even folded some laundry without prompting from Mom. The spell the monster cast had allowed her to enjoy a rare quiet night of sleep. With Loretta moving about the room, Spark needed to remain still.

At 8:39 in the morning, Mom called for Matthew. He did not answer. She went to his room, knocked on the door. Still nothing. After peeking inside, Mom marched over to Loretta's room.

"Where's Matthew?"

Loretta removed her headphones. "I don't know."

It went on for another hour. *Where's Matthew? Matthew? Matthew! Where would he be?* When they called his phone, they heard it ringing on the dresser beside his bed. At one point, Mom and Dad argued over whether Matthew had joined some new club at school that met on Sundays. Meanwhile, Loretta sat at her desk, with one headphone on her left ear, the other pulled away so she could listen to her parents. Twice they entered the room and asked where Matthew could have gone. Twice she said she didn't know.

Spark had never felt so helpless.

By eleven a.m., after frantically dialing everyone who could have known Matthew's whereabouts, Mom and Dad stood in the living room and argued over whether they should call the police.

Realizing that Loretta might hear, Mom whispered to Dad. "I'm not taking any chances," she said. "I'm not. Not after Sofia."

At this point, Loretta dropped her headphones on her desk and went downstairs. Spark could not hear what followed. Loretta spoke in whispers. When Mom shouted "What?" Spark knew that Loretta had told them about Matthew's plan to search for Sofia himself. And that's when things went really crazy.

Mom called 911. "You don't need to do that," Loretta said. "I bet he'll be back this afternoon. He's just being all dramatic."

"He left his phone," Mom said.

"Right. Now you can't track him."

"He could get hurt!"

"He can get around fine, Mom. You guys treat him like a baby sometimes."

The operator asked Mom to explain her emergency. "I'd like to report a missing child," Mom said. She took the phone into another room.

"He left his leg brace," Dad said.

"He can get around without a leg brace," Loretta said.

Within minutes, police cars clogged the driveway, each with a row of blue and red lights on top and a golden shield painted on the side. Two officers arrived to take a statement. Then a detective parked his silver BMW in front of the house. He was a pale man with a pencil mustache and a charcoal suit that was a size too big. He wore a police badge on a chain around his neck.

Dad led the police to Matthew's room so they could snoop around. Spark could hear the tension in their voices rising. The officers asked the same questions over and over. Mom and Dad answered them again and again. Every few minutes, Mom asked when they would start combing the neighborhood. "You have his photo, so start looking!"

"Ma'am, we need a little more information first," the detective said. And then he asked the same questions that the other cops had asked already.

The whole time, Loretta sat on her bed, hugging her knees in close, while her phone blinked and buzzed with new text messages. Clearly, word had gotten around the neighborhood about the cops at the house. Darcy and Jisha and all the rest chimed in, asking for updates. At a certain point, Loretta stopped tapping the screen, and the messages stacked on top of each other like little flashing bricks.

Loretta remained still even after the inevitable knock on her door. Mom came in and sat on the bed. "I know it's annoying, but the police asked to search your room," she said.

The detective waited in the doorway.

"Mom . . ."

"I know," Mom said. "I know. Please just do this for me, okay? Please?"

Instead of fighting, Loretta climbed off the bed and walked out, brushing past the detective. Mom followed her. While Loretta pouted in the hallway, the cops rummaged through the drawers and poked around in the closet. As he checked the shelf, the detective lifted Spark by her collar, smirked, and then returned her to her spot.

The man took note of the row of movie posters on the wall. "Loretta, come here," he said.

She entered the room, her head lowered.

"Which of these is your favorite?" the detective asked.

She pointed to the poster for *The Empire Strikes Back*. Darth Vader's black helmet occupied most of the image.

"Why?"

"Because my brother and I watch it every Christmas Eve."

"That's not a Christmas movie."

"Yes it is." She watched it on Christmas, so it was a Christmas movie. End of discussion.

The detective decided not to press her on it. He stepped into the hall, and as he tried to thank her for her cooperation, Loretta closed the door in his face.

She grabbed her phone and sat on the carpet with her back against the door, like a barricade. With her thumbs tapping furiously, she descended into a trance, brought on by texts and posts and updates. Spark did not like it when she did this, though in this case she understood why.

Downstairs, the chairs slid on the linoleum as the grown-ups gathered at the kitchen table. They whispered too low for

Spark to hear. The voices became like distant, rumbling storms, the kind that would have frightened Loretta years earlier. When Mom started to cry, Loretta could no longer hide from what was happening. The phone dropped from her hand, falling between her knees with a thud. She covered her ears and clenched her jaw. Tears ran to the tip of her nose and fell off, one by one, until at last she pounded her fist on the ground and stood.

Loretta charged down the steps to the kitchen. The detective immediately stopped talking.

"Give us a minute, Loretta," Dad said.

"No! I'm sitting here, too."

"Loretta—"

"I said I'm sitting here!"

Dad tried to repeat himself. Loretta would not allow him to finish his sentence.

"Don't tell me what to do!" she yelled. "He's my brother! I want to know what's going on!"

"You need to calm down—"

"Derek," Mom said, in a soothing tone she used only when someone was scared or hurt. "Derek, it's okay. She can join us."

In the awkward silence, one of the officers chuckled at the audacity of this little girl. He tried to cover it with a fake cough.

The detective continued, going over next steps in the search. They would search the same places where Sofia may have gone. And they would question people at the school, starting with Matthew's classmates.

When he finished, the chairs in the kitchen moved again as the officers left. The voices died out. Mom cried a little. Dad did, too, though he made it sound as if he was clearing his throat.

With a trembling voice, Mom said that they were going to drive around the neighborhood. Maybe they would get lucky and spot Matthew. If nothing else, it would pass the time while the police did their work. "We'll play some of your music, too," Mom said to Loretta, with a hint of desperation. "You can plug in your phone thing."

If Loretta answered, Spark could not hear it.

The family left shortly after. Spark could finally move. And this time, she knew exactly where to go.

TEN

Leaning on the window frame, Spark unspooled a string of purple yarn. The glass tilted outward, creating enough space for her to squeeze through. Once outside, she would climb along the gutter to Matthew's room. With the door locked, the only way to see inside was from the window.

Even with the family gone for now, Zed insisted on keeping watch at the door.

"You've really gone crazy this time," he said.

Despite his enormous ears, Zed swore that he hadn't heard the ruckus from the night before. Spark believed him. Whatever magic this monster used to keep quiet, it seemed to work on everyone. Except bears.

"I heard what happened in Matthew's room," she said. "Wherever they went, it was up."

To the attic, then. Start there, work her way to the roof.

"But you heard Loretta, right?" Zed said. "Matthew went looking for his friend."

"She's wrong. And for all we know, that's exactly what this monster wants us to believe."

Spark unclasped her collar and slipped it through the spool of yarn. She then fastened the collar so that it sat across her chest, from her shoulder to her side. The spool would unroll as she climbed, keeping her connected to the safety of the bedroom in case anything went wrong. At the same time, the collar would act as a scabbard for Arctos. She slipped the blade in, fitting it snugly against her fur. As long as she didn't make any sudden movements, it would not cut her. This really *is* crazy, she thought. But then she caught a glimpse of the claw mark on the movie poster. She did not have time to wait for everyone else to understand what was happening in this house.

She tied the other end of the yarn to the lever that opened the window. Outside, clouds rolled in, carrying a chilly breeze. Spark would have to act quickly before a storm arrived. The neighbor's driveway was empty, and only a few dog walkers and joggers passed by on the street. None of them glanced at the top of the house.

As she pushed through the window, she heard Zed whimper in that monkey voice of his. Spark climbed to the top of the window frame and stretched her paw to the gutter. The metal squeaked a little, but it held her weight. Above, the roof formed a triangle against the white sky. In the center, the circular window of the attic faced out like the eye of a cyclops.

Hanging off the gutter, Spark worked her way along with the yarn unwinding below her. When she reached Matthew's window, she dropped to the sill, scaring off a bumblebee. She cupped her paws around her eyes and peered inside. The sheet lay twisted on the bed, and a few of the storyboard papers had fallen to the floor. The closet door hung open, with a pile of shoes threatening to tumble over. A monster attack could do little to change the clutter in Matthew's room.

"Do you see anything?" Zed shouted.

She waited for the wind to die down before answering. "No one's in there."

Zed was supposed to be looking out, but he must have panicked when Spark took too long. Typical sock monkey. No discipline.

Spark glanced at the circular window of the attic above. Even more so than before, it appeared as a giant eye, rolling in its socket and watching her. Taunting her. A monster in its own right.

"A test," she said.

She remembered what Rana told her on that long-ago night. *To be honest with you, little bear: either you can or you can't. There's no teaching it.*

Spark began to climb. The spool of yarn spun on her back.

"Where are you going?" Zed yelled.

"I told you! The attic!"

"No!"

The wind drowned out his voice. Just as well. She needed to keep going, with no distractions, before she changed her mind.

To pass the time, Spark recited the Founders' oath. She found it much easier to recall without a giant monster looming over her.

"We serve goodness and truth," she said as she climbed onto the next tier of the roof. "We give refuge to the innocent—"

Something skittered along the shingles to her left. She turned. A furry creature raised on its haunches before her. It was another squirrel. No, it was the *same* squirrel from the day before. The skinny one. He flicked his tail in a show of dominance.

"You again," Spark said.

This time, the squirrel stood his ground. Spark growled at him. The squirrel flinched. Spark screamed, this time flapping her arms. The squirrel recoiled and ran away, vanishing over the other side of the roof.

"Great, I'm teaching a squirrel how to be brave," she said.

Spark continued her ascent to the top tier, still muttering the oath. When she made it to the part about the final light, she arrived at the base of the attic window, where she pressed her paw on the cool glass. The frame tilted inward on two hinges, releasing a musty scent. Inside, she saw a circle of light on the hardwood floor, with her tiny shadow in the lower corner of it. At the opposite end of the room, the other circular window hung in the darkness like a full moon. The walls formed a triangle, tall enough in the center for an adult to stand upright. Cardboard boxes lined the walls, resembling the skyline of an abandoned city. Old coats hung from a rack near the staircase. A fake Christmas tree poked out of a crate, still covered in tinsel.

Spark called Sir Reginald's name. Nothing stirred.

She did not want to go inside. But she had come this far. And so much was at stake.

"Zed!" she yelled. "Can you hear me?"

"Yes!"

"If I pull on this yarn, you pull me back. Got it?"

"Got it!"

Spark rolled over the window frame and tumbled inside, landing on a cardboard box filled with Halloween decorations. A great cloud of dust lifted from the box, engulfing her. Holding the yarn, ready to tug it at the first sign of trouble, Spark jumped to the floor. The boxes rose high all around her, like the walls of a canyon. Behind her, a breeze tilted the window frame, making it squeak. Spark kept moving. She would try to make it to the other wall before returning to the window. If she did not see Sir Reginald, then he either was not here or did not wish to be found.

After passing the coat rack, she arrived at a box lying on its side, blocking her path. Picture frames had fallen out of it, along with a pair of candleholders and a little angel statue with one of its wings broken off.

Spark heard something: a metallic click. She froze.

"Hello?"

Something shuffled on the other side of the box. Spark could hear an object scraping against the floor. The vibration rumbled in the pads of her feet. She remembered the monster's claws. Is this where he lived? Is this where he waited until dark? She braced herself, crouching in a fighting stance but ready to run if necessary.

A shiny piece of metal emerged from behind the box. A Swiss Army knife. A furry black paw held the handle. And then the creature stepped into view: a squat little thing, with round ears, dark eyes, a square jaw.

She would have recognized Sir Reginald anywhere. But he did not recognize her. He lifted the handle and unlatched a second blade from the bottom, transforming the knife into a double-edged spear. As he approached, Spark noticed a huge gash in his side. His innards were nothing more than yarn, an enormous bundle of brown thread that trailed behind him. And his left foot dragged along the floor, nearly cut off. More yarn fell out of the wound.

"Sir Reginald, it's me. It's—"

The old bear swung the blade. Spark dodged it easily. The point got stuck in the wood. Sir Reginald pried it free and swung the other end. Spark ducked underneath and side-stepped another lazy swipe. She reached for Arctos, but then decided against it. Sir Reginald could hardly move, and here he was picking a fight with a younger bear. The one he trained, no less.

Having seen enough, Spark waited for Sir Reginald to hold the blade level at his chest. When he did, she grabbed hold of it. Sir Reginald tried to wrestle it away, but Spark used her weight to drive him backward. He tripped over his innards and fell over. She pinned him, pressing the handle to his neck.

"It's me," she said.

Sir Reginald loosened his grip. "Hotshot!" he said. After all these years, he still used that sarcastic nickname whenever she showed off or acted as if she knew everything. She never liked it. But this time, hearing it made her feel better.

"Oh, no, Hotshot. Forgive me."

"What happened, Sir?"

He clenched his eyes shut and turned away from her. "I failed."

It broke her heart to hear him say it. The proud bear, her mentor, reduced to this.

"You didn't fail," she said. "You hear me? You didn't fail."

"He took Matthew."

She let go of the knife. "I know. He wants Loretta next."

"I was so arrogant. I thought the monster would see me and run away."

She could not blame him. Monsters were supposed to run away from teddy bears.

Sir Reginald struggled to his feet. "We have to get moving."

"Wait. You're hurt."

"I am fine." He picked up a clump of the yarn that spilled from his side.

"Let me fix you. We can't do anything until you're better."

For years, Sir Reginald lectured her on how to be a good protector. He had never shown a sign of weakness before. He never doubted himself. And so it must have hurt him deeply to quietly sit there, holding his stuffing in his paws. He gazed at her, frustrated but hopeful.

"Get to it, Hotshot."

ELEVEN

After removing her heavy collar, Spark used Arctos to cut the yarn from the spool. Upon returning to Loretta's room, she would snip the line that was still tied to the window and let it drift away in the wind.

She rummaged through the drawers of a sewing desk until she found a needle and thread. "Is blue okay?" she asked. Sir Reginald said yes.

While Spark threaded the needle, Sir Reginald rested on his side, exposing the wound. Spark gathered the yarn in both paws and stuffed it back inside him. The old bear grunted and growled while she did it. She wondered what had gone through his mind while he was trapped here. He must have given in to despair, wondering what he could have done differently to save Matthew. It could happen to anyone. Anyone could lose hope in dark moments like this. Only the brave and the lucky could ever find it again.

She tried to distract him by asking boring questions. "Are we all stuffed with yarn?"

"No," he said. "Most of us have cotton inside."

"Why are you different?"

"The person who made me must have had some extra yarn lying around."

"*Who* made you?"

"This again," he grumbled.

She knew what he would say next, but she found comfort in hearing it again.

"It does not matter who made us," he said. "What matters is what we do *now*."

Bears never remembered being made. They only remembered meeting their dusa for the first time. "That is when life begins," Sir Reginald often said. "That is when we find our purpose."

Every once in a while, Spark still asked Sir Reginald what would happen to them once the children became adults. He always waved her off. "The code says, 'Always and forever,'" he would say. "If you are brave, if you do your duty, the Grand Sleuth will call on you when the time is right. Or perhaps you will watch over Loretta's child, the way I watch over Matthew now. We go where we are needed."

She decided not to bug him about it this time.

The surgery began with the foot. When Spark brandished the needle, Sir Reginald turned away. She pierced the edge of the wound and slid the metal through. The thread pulled the two sides of the hole together. She continued like this, again and again, crisscrossing the thread each time. Before long, a chain of tiny blue Xs lined Sir Reginald's ankle, like some strange tattoo.

Spark moved on to the hole in his side. "I need to know what you saw," she said. "The night Matthew disappeared."

Like a sock monkey, Sir Reginald covered his eyes with his paws. Under normal circumstances, she would have given him more time. But circumstances were hardly normal. And they had no time.

Sir Reginald let his paws fall away. He stared at the ceiling.

"I have heard stories about this monster," he said. "At least . . . I thought they were stories. Meant to scare me. I never did that to you, by the way. I never made anything up."

"I know." Spark fastened another X before starting on the next.

Sir Reginald patted the stitches on his side. "They call him Jakmal. And he is using a scratcher."

"I'm sorry—what?"

"I have told you before what a scratcher is," he said. "It is a machine. Or some kind of magic thing—it does not matter. It is a device that can carve a hole into our world."

Spark remembered the gaping chasm in the corner of Loretta's room. "Yes, that's what I saw. A big hole leading to . . . somewhere."

"He comes and goes as he pleases," Sir Reginald said. "But the holes are unstable. They are more like bubbles. They float where they will. Their edges can wobble and break. And at those edges, you can be halfway in our world and halfway in his."

"That is how I ended up in the chimney."

"The chimney," Spark repeated, no longer shocked by anything he said.

Sir Reginald took a deep breath. And then he told her everything. Jakmal had first appeared in Matthew's room the same night he tried to take Loretta. The monster laid a trap for the old bear. When Sir Reginald tried to chase him away, he fell through a portal and reappeared in the chimney, which Dad had plastered shut years before. It took Sir Reginald an entire day to wedge his way out and make it back to Matthew's room.

He returned to his spot in Matthew's closet just in time for Jakmal's next attack. It began with a strange breeze wafting across the room, like mist. A great void opened in the corner. When Jakmal emerged, Sir Reginald knew right away that he had come for the boy. The bear lunged at the intruder, knowing it was a lost cause, but still hoping to buy some time. The monster slashed at him, tossing him against the wall. Using the pincer on the end of his tail, Jakmal lifted Matthew from the bed. Matthew awoke, delirious, shouting for his parents.

"Jakmal used a spell, didn't he?" Spark asked. "So the humans wouldn't hear."

"Precisely," Sir Reginald said. "A muffle, I have heard it called. It worked."

Wounded but still angry, Sir Reginald jumped on the monster's head, cocked his arm, and punched him right in the eye. The creature screamed.

"Remember that," Sir Reginald told Spark. "Remember that we can make him scream."

As the monster slithered away, Sir Reginald fell to the floor. Desperate, the bear grabbed the boy's lamp and threw it into the void. With the cord still plugged in to the socket, the rift could not seal itself. Instead, it moved along the wall to the ceiling. When the cord came unplugged, Sir Reginald grabbed it and found himself lifted from the ground, toward this moving doorway to another world. He would follow this creature into the darkness if he had to. As he neared the opening, he saw Jakmal's home: a towering castle glowing red with torches. One of the torches hurtled toward him. He realized too late that it was the lamp. Jakmal must have thrown it in anger.

Sir Reginald let go of the cord and fell. The next thing he knew, he was on the other side of the ceiling, in the attic. He had passed through the portal, but not in time to follow the monster. Even worse: his foot was stuck in the floorboard. Kneeling in a pile of his yarn, he wept. His best friend in the world was gone, and there was nothing he could do about it.

"It took me a while to find the courage to cut off my foot," Sir Reginald said. "By then, I figured it was too late. I might as well stay here with the other discarded toys."

Spark imagined him fused to the floor, his face frozen in terror.

"I've never heard of a monster that could do this," she said. "That could take a child into their world. At least, not for a hundred years or more."

"I have," Sir Reginald said. "When I was Dad's bear, in Grandma's house."

The story came from a one-eyed bear named Vincent, who protected Dad's sister. Vincent heard the story from another bear, who heard it from another, and so on.

"From what I saw, Vincent got most of it right."

Spark pulled the thread until it tugged the wound closed.

"Tell me," Spark said. "Tell me everything you know."

TWELVE

There was a time, long before the League of Ursus, when monsters filled the skies. When they stalked the forests. When they crept in every shadow. Children would go missing in those days. Entire villages would lose all of their young ones in a single night. There would be a scraping of claws against the doors, a screech and a howl, a child's cry for help, and then a great flapping of wings as the monsters made off with their prey. The adults blamed one another, not seeing the danger right in front of their faces. They would not listen to the children, the only ones who knew what was happening.

A handful of brave warriors at last took a stand. Bears, of course. The strongest among them, a little grizzly, became the leader. The general, they called her. Her dusa was the daughter of the village chief, a girl who would one day become chief herself. The monsters knew that taking this child would break the town's leaders. If that ever happened, the adults would start handing their children over in order to make the monsters go away. A sacrifice. It had happened before.

At the general's side stood her second-in-command, a furry brown bear whose dusa would sometimes play with the chief's daughter. He possessed the ability, rare among his kind, to cast spells that could distract or even blind the demons, but he had yet to master his skills. This wizard—hexen was the word they used—pledged his loyalty to the general, along with the others. Each of them looked the others in the eye and said, "You have my sword and my life." They called this group a juro, a fellowship of bears. Bears who gathered in a juro would repeat these sacred words, sealing their bond until the monsters were gone.

Meanwhile, the other friends of the humans refused to fight. Even the toy soldiers cowered, hoping to save only themselves.

And so, in the middle of the night, the bears gathered at the edge of the village. Their dusas hid in the houses behind them. The parents tried to sleep, but nightmares kept them awake.

The monsters arrived as a great cloud, a wave of flapping wings in the sky. Manglers, they were called. Nasty, razor-toothed beasts with leathery wings and spiked tails. They circled the town, their jaws snapping, claws grasping. They snarled and spat. The bears held their ground, each gripping a spear and a torch.

The cloud swirled overhead like a tornado and then came roaring down on the bears. A terrible battle broke out. Through the night, blades slashed at the marauding demons. The bears were scattered, each fighting alone, hoping to survive the night. And then, a war cry startled the manglers. One of them was so terrified that he let go of the bear he held, letting him flop onto the dirt.

Two knights charged into the fray. They wore gleaming golden armor and shiny helmets with spikes on top. Their swords reflected the firelight as they tore through their enemies. Taken by surprise, the demons retreated. They ascended into the sky like a flight of birds.

The battle won, the bears turned to their new allies.

"Who are you?" the general asked.

"Friends," the first knight said. His voice sounded like distant thunder.

The two knights resembled humans, but they were something else. Their skin glowed. They were each stronger than a dozen men. Their armor and swords were flawless.

The first knight introduced himself as Jak. "This is my brother," he said, pointing to the silent one.

"And what is your name?" the general asked the second knight.

The brother remained silent, with the visor of his helmet shielding his eyes.

The general asked where they came from.

"We all come from the same place," the knight said. "From the minds of children."

The bears looked at each other.

"But you are not a toy, nor a doll," the general said.

"The boy we watch over—only he can see us."

"I do not understand."

"They are imaginary friends," the hexen said. "But they are also . . . real."

"Yes," the knight said.

"That is impossible," the general said.

The knight laughed. His brother merely smiled. "A bear made of cloth, with buttons for eyes, dares to tell me what is impossible!"

"Children sometimes have imaginary friends, it is true," the general said. "But none of them have ever come to life."

"Some children are special. Perhaps they have the same magic as your witch."

"I am a hexen," the brown bear said. He demanded to know who this child was, the one with the power to create this knight with their mind. The knights refused to tell him.

"It does not matter," the general said. "The monsters will return tomorrow. Will you fight with us?"

The knights rose from their seats. The first one held out his gloved hand. "What is it you say? 'I pledge you my sword and my life.'"

The general shook his hand. A new alliance had been formed.

But nearby, the hexen stood with his arms folded, his brow furrowed.

The next night, the bears left their dusas and gathered once more. Holding their torches and spears, the warriors kept watch. The breeze made the flames dance but did not carry the sounds of the enemy. Not yet.

The hexen approached the general. "Ma'am, will the knights return?"

"I believe so."

The hexen grew uneasy.

"What troubles you?" the general asked.

"They say that they are imaginary friends. That a child conjured them somehow. Out of thin air!"

"They conjure *us*, do they not?" the general said.

"It is not the same," the hexen said. "No one can be trusted with that kind of power. And what if the manglers could harness that magic? They could summon more of their kind. No one would be able to stop them."

"True," the general said. "But perhaps the world needs more children like this. To fight the darkness."

The hexen pleaded with her. "I do not trust the knights. Something is terribly wrong with all of this."

"They saved us last night."

"It could be a trap. They know that we need reinforcements now."

The general valued her hexen's advice. But they had no choice.

"I am the leader of this juro," the general said. "I have made my decision."

When the knights arrived, their golden armor gleaming like the sunrise, the bears gathered around them. A few of the bears even reached out their paws to touch their boots, to make sure they were real. At the edge of the circle, the hexen sharpened his little sword, as if he had not noticed their arrival.

When the church bells struck midnight, the wind carried the sound of shrieking. The warriors readied their weapons. The great cloud of monsters appeared on the horizon, twice as big as the night before, blotting out the moon. Instead of circling the village, the manglers swooped in immediately, moving so quickly that they snuffed out the bears' torches. The juro fought in the darkness, slashing and cutting through the horde of monsters.

The two knights worked together, fighting back-to-back so that no one could sneak up behind them. One brother would pin a mangler in the dirt, the other would slash it with his sword. In a frenzy, the monsters regrouped and surrounded the knights, knocking them to the ground. The bears tried to help, but the monsters fought them off.

At the edge of the battle, the hexen chanted the words of a new spell, one he had never tried before. He pointed his paws at the manglers surrounding the knights and shouted the words. An enormous ball of flame appeared, so bright that everyone, bear and monster alike, shielded their eyes. The explosion sent several of the monsters flying across the dirt, their wings torn and burned. In the chaos that followed, the bears chased away those that remained.

As the enemy retreated, the bears formed a ring around the fallen warriors. In the center, the first knight held his brother, who lay dying. The general ordered the hexen to help them—to cast a healing spell of some kind.

The hexen placed his paws on the two brothers. He whispered words that no one had ever heard before.

The silent knight slumped over. His brother held him, weeping. And then, his voice deepened. He grunted like one of the monsters. He clutched at his throat, his body shaking with horrible pain. The bears backed away.

The general, realizing too late that the hexen had somehow cursed the knights, pleaded with him to stop.

"We are getting rid of *all* the monsters tonight," the hexen said.

The knight tore his armor off. His face turned white. His skin bubbled like the surface of boiling water. Two horns sprouted from his forehead. He hunched on all fours like an animal and ran into the forest.

The bears stood silently. A breeze drifted through the forest and then died out.

THIRTEEN

Sir Reginald allowed his last words hang in the air for a moment.

"How could a bear do something like that?" Spark said.

"He convinced himself that he was right, and that everyone was against him," Sir Reginald said. "It can be impossible to change a person's mind after that."

In spite of the hexen's treachery, the bears' plan worked. Word spread of their battle. For the first time, the tables had turned. The monsters were afraid. And they knew to stay away.

"But to betray another warrior like that . . . ," Spark said. "What was the hexen's punishment?"

"No one knows. The League was not around yet. Their names are lost."

"It must have been terrible," Spark said. "For the knight to leave his brother behind."

Sir Reginald nodded.

"But why go after Matthew and Loretta?" Spark asked. "Why now?"

"Like I said. Some children have this ability to conjure things from their imagination. And our dusas happen to be born storytellers. Maybe they can even break the hexen's curse."

"Do you believe they have that kind of power?"

"No. But Jakmal might."

Spark thought for a moment. "Maybe the film contest is what made the monster come looking for them."

"That is possible. The children's love gives us strength. And in return, we protect them. But perhaps this love acts like a beacon for someone like Jakmal."

It was a relief to hear Sir Reginald talking about their mission. Even when she became raggedy and worn out like him, she would need to hear these things. To keep her going.

"We must hurry," Sir Reginald said. "The beast gathers strength every day."

Spark shuddered. "Do you think that Matthew . . ."

He raised his paw to silence her. Neither of them wanted to say it. What was a bear without a dusa?

"It is not too late for Loretta," he said.

"Don't say it like that." But then Spark thought, how *should* he say it? It made sense. She was prepared to fight a monster, but not prepared to lose to one.

"It gets worse," he said. "This castle that Jakmal calls home—it is very dangerous."

Sir Reginald described the fortress: a long, narrow structure, with turrets and windows, rising from the foot of a volcano. A moat filled with lava surrounded it on all sides.

"I believe the castle is some kind of gateway," he said.

"To where?"

"Everywhere. My guess is that he has punched holes all over this town. No one is safe."

Sir Reginald explained how the portals worked: the scratcher opened them, and the castle kept them stable. Without the fortress's sturdy walls, forged by magic, the portals could expand too far, like a zipper bursting open. They could wipe out an entire city, or something even bigger. That was why Jakmal used the scratcher in such a remote place. By housing the portals inside, the lair became a labyrinth of doorways, and the monster held the key. Spark imagined portals opening in schools, in parks, scooping children away and hiding them. Creating an ocean of fear that would only make Jakmal stronger.

"It takes a special kind of power to use the scratcher," Sir Reginald said.

"Like the kind of power the child in your story had?"

"I suppose. Destroying that device must be our top priority."

The old bear lifted his head to check Spark's progress with the stitches. A few more loops to go. Spark tied the last stitch and bit off the end of the thread. Sir Reginald patted the wound tenderly, trying to brush the fur over it to conceal the bright thread. Standing, he put weight on his repaired foot. Spark held out her paws to hold him steady, but after a few steps he no longer needed her.

"I painted the alarm signal on the side of the house," Spark said. "How long will it take for the Grand Sleuth to respond?"

"I cannot say. We may not be the only bears asking for help."

The thought made Spark shudder.

"We have trained for this," Sir Reginald said. "We must

focus on what we can do, not on waiting for rescue."

Walking with more confidence now, he headed straight for Arctos, which lay atop Spark's collar. He gripped the handle and lifted the blade to eye level. A shard of reflected light swiped across his face. Despite what had happened, he was still Sir Reginald the Brave.

He asked if Spark could get him to Matthew's room. She told him that the door was locked.

"Put me in the linen closet then."

When Spark objected, he reminded her that he had hid there once before—when Matthew went to the hospital with a bad fever, many years earlier. He tried to follow him as Dad carried the boy away. Trapped out in the open, Sir Reginald took shelter in the closet until the coast was clear.

At the attic door, Spark climbed on his shoulders and reached for the latch to unlock it. The door creaked open, letting in a warm breeze.

"Thank you for finding me," he said.

She knew what he meant. He could have stayed in the attic for years, defeated and filled with regret. She brought him back to the land of the living, where he could still make a difference. A new chance at life.

"I have to tell you something," Spark said. "I got lazy. I was so happy to be needed again that I stopped keeping watch. Never again. From here on, we're going to make up for our mistakes."

Sir Reginald held her paw and squeezed it.

Spark adjusted her collar and looked at him. "Now let's get to work."

FOURTEEN

The bears parted ways in the hall. Sir Reginald entered the linen closet and crouched behind a stack of towels. "Find me tonight," he said as Spark shut the door on him. "I shall think of something by then."

Spark returned to Loretta's room. It seemed so much smaller now, frozen in time, like an image in a photo album. When Zed saw her, he leapt from the shelf and gave her a big hug.

"You cut the cord!" he said.

"Sorry. I didn't mean to scare you."

"Did you find him?"

"Yes. He's safe, in the linen closet."

Zed asked if Sir Reginald had seen the monster. Spark gave him the bare details, not wanting to frighten him any further. Sir Reginald tried to fight the beast, but it fled with Matthew and left the bear stranded in the attic. End of story.

Before Zed could ask anything else, Spark said she needed to cut the string tied to the window before someone found it. But as she mounted the windowsill, she heard the front door of the house slam shut. The family was home earlier than expected. Spark waved at Zed to get back in his spot before racing up the shelves herself.

Instead of going straight to her room, Loretta paused at the top of the stairs, then crept through the hall, toward Matthew's door. She tried to be completely silent, but it was no use. Spark could hear the sound of metal scraping. Then the door to Matthew's room clicked open. So Loretta knew how to pick a lock! Of course she did. A minute later, she entered her room with the camera and tripod. She planted it in the middle of the carpet and aimed it at the spot where the monster had appeared. Ah, so that was her plan: to catch the monster on video. She tried the same thing with Santa Claus a few years before, with no success.

The way Loretta was acting unsettled Spark. The girl worked methodically, her lips pursed. She hardly even blinked. To make room for the tripod, she kicked aside a shoe that had found its way onto the carpet. She must have spent all of her emotions already, and all that remained was an urgent desire to make sense of what was happening.

Somewhere downstairs, the phone rang.

"Loretta!" Mom called. "Darcy's on the phone."

"I'll take it up here."

Loretta went into her parents' room and grabbed the wireless. "Hello?"

Darcy mumbled on the other end. Loretta returned to her room with the phone perched on her shoulder.

"I'm sorry," she said in a wooden tone of voice. "I just didn't feel like answering my cell."

The two girls shared so many secrets that they could speak in their own language. Granted, most of the language consisted of grunts and murmurs, but Spark enjoyed listening to it. Even when Loretta shrugged or rolled her eyes, Darcy seemed to hear it through the phone. Sometimes, Darcy would pour her heart out about some boy, or a teacher they didn't like, and Loretta would listen. On many occasions, Loretta assured Darcy with a simple phrase: "I'm your friend." It was like her very own code of the League of Ursus.

On this day, Spark tried to listen but could make out only a few words. Darcy's voice wavered—she was trying to figure out how to ask something. After nodding and saying *uh-huh* for a few minutes, Loretta finally cut her off.

"We can't do the movie," she said. "We just can't, okay?"

Loretta winced when she said it. In response, Darcy said something reassuring. Of course they couldn't shoot the movie now, not with all this insanity around them.

With the phone pressed to her ear, Loretta peered into the camera's viewfinder. "We'll talk at lunch on Tuesday," she said. Darcy asked why she wasn't going to school tomorrow. "We're doing another search," Loretta replied. "My mom wanted me to go to school, but I was like, 'No way, I'm going with you.'"

They both took turns complaining about their parents. Probably because it felt normal. When they were finished, they said goodbye. And as soon as she switched off the phone, Loretta burst into tears. She could maintain her stony detective act for only so long. She snatched Spark from her resting spot, fell on the bed, and wrapped her arms around the bear's neck. Loretta cried so hard that her body shook and she gasped for breath.

Without moving her head, Spark glanced at Zed on the shelf. The monkey leaned against the wall, a sad little lump of cloth and stuffing.

Spark wanted to break the rules, tell her friend that everything would be all right. Instead, she let the girl hold her while she mouthed the Founders' code of the League of Ursus again and again.

Bears serve.

Bears watch.

Bears protect.

Always and forever.

FIFTEEN

That night, a heavy rainstorm rolled over the neighborhood. Mom and Dad stayed up late whispering about what to do next. At that point, they were beyond tired, beyond sleep. They tried to reach Sofia's dad, but the call went to voicemail every time. Then they spent an hour trying to find a private detective online, but no one would answer the phone. Mom said it would be best to have as many people as possible looking for Matthew, while Dad thought that the police could handle it.

Meanwhile, Loretta texted nearly every single person she knew, all while searching on her computer for facts and theories about people who went missing. With the lights off, the glow from the screens made Loretta look like a ghost. Her eyelids drooped lower with each text she received.

She closed the laptop and seemed ready for bed. But then she opened it again and started searching for the kinds of things that Matthew mentioned when they talked about Sofia. Terms like *demon, forces of darkness, hauntings*. She found a page that featured nothing but old paintings of goblins and witches carrying children from their beds and slinking away. The creatures seemed giddy as they hauled off their prey, while the children often screamed, or sometimes appeared completely bewildered by their fate. Loretta kept scrolling and scrolling, and the images would not stop. Hundreds of people, over hundreds of years, had felt compelled to recreate these monsters in stories and art. When she couldn't take it anymore, Loretta closed the computer, leaned on her elbows, and covered her mouth with her hands.

Beside her, the phone buzzed with another text message, this one from Claire. "O my god I heard so sorry!" it said. "Call u tomorrow! ♥ ♥ ♥"

Long after the family grew exhausted and went to sleep, the wind rattled the walls, and heavy drops of rain splashed on the roof. The purple string, still tied to the handle on the window, whipped against the glass. The noise provided cover for Spark as she dropped from the mattress and sneaked under the tripod. Above her, the camera rolled, its red light hovering over the floor. For once, Spark wished that her dusa were not so clever and curious. Jakmal would never allow himself to get caught on one of the humans' recording devices. He would find another way into the room, while Spark would have to avoid the camera at all costs.

In the linen closet, Sir Reginald crawled out from under a heap of towels. He rubbed his shoulder and bent his knees to regain some flexibility. Spark felt instant relief upon seeing him. One bear became two—maybe not enough to fight off Jakmal, but enough to make him regret coming anywhere near this house.

"I want to show you something," Sir Reginald said.

"I'd rather wait in Loretta's room."

"Listen," he said. "I can smell the scratcher. I have been smelling it all day."

"Go on."

"It smells like oil and soot. And rust. Matthew's room was covered with it the day Jakmal took him. Did you notice it?"

Spark remembered: the monster carried the scent of grease on him.

"Come here," he said. "Let me show you."

Sir Reginald burrowed under the towels. Spark followed him until she reached the corner of the closet. He pressed his snout to the molding and inhaled. He motioned for her to try it. Through the seams in the hardwood floor, she detected the scent.

"You see?" Sir Reginald said. "It is moving downstairs."

"You want to go down there? And leave Loretta here?"

"We need to know his pattern. We need to know where he feels safe in this house. And where he does *not* feel safe."

Spark watched him without responding.

"This might be our chance to see what he is doing," Sir Reginald said. "I have never smelled it so strong before."

Something heavy and hard hit the floor downstairs, almost directly below them. Spark jumped at the sound. "Okay," she said, shaking. "We'll go."

On their way to the staircase, Spark checked on Loretta. She sniffed for the metallic odor and found nothing out of the ordinary, only the detergent on the freshly laundered sheets. On the bed, Loretta slept with her hair tumbled over her face, her mouth open.

The two bears tiptoed along the railing. The streetlamps cast an eerie light through the windows. Part of the living room rug and the bookcase were visible, leaving everything else cloaked in shadow. At the foot of the stairs, the noise from the rain grew louder, like a steady beating of thousands of footsteps on the roof. Spark and Sir Reginald crept side by side toward the front door of the house.

The scent grew stronger, making her nose twitch.

She stopped. Something was wrong. The door stood slightly open, allowing a sliver of light to squeeze through.

A gust of wind whistled through the crack. If not for the welcome mat barring the way, the door would have flung open.

She glanced at Sir Reginald for an explanation. He had none. Mom and Dad locked the house every night. After sealing all three entrances, one of them would flick on the sensor light, which glowed brightly whenever a squirrel or fox ran across the yard.

Spark stepped outside. Above, the overhang of the roof kept the front steps dry. Still, the rain battered the driveway so hard that it created a mist. A breeze rustled the tree on the neighbor's lawn. And with it came the scent again, thick and wet like the rain.

"Do you see anything?" Sir Reginald asked.

Spark shook her head no. Her nose continued to twitch on its own, leading her farther outside into the damp air. Tiny droplets stuck to her fur.

"Wait," Sir Reginald said.

The door clapped shut. Spark turned. Her gaze drifted to the roof, where an enormous dark form clung to the edge of the gutter, like some oversized termites' nest. With the rain dancing all around it, the form moved. The head lifted, revealing owl-like eyes and glistening fangs. Taking his time—perhaps to mock her—the creature crawled down the side of the house, grunting each time his claw landed.

And there was no denying it: he was *bigger* this time. And the horns on his head had grown longer.

Jakmal hissed.

Panicked, Spark ran along the side of the house. The rain soaked her. Her sodden feet splashed in the puddles. She instantly felt heavier and slower. While she ran between the house and the parked car, Jakmal leapt on top of the vehicle, caving in the hood and windshield. *Kaaa-roooom.* Broken glass tinkled on the asphalt. Spark rounded the corner, hoping to get inside through the back door. But when she jumped onto the knob, her paws slid right off. Above, a light went on in Mom and Dad's room, like an eye blinking awake.

Jakmal poked his head around the side of the building, still hissing. The rain dripped from his chin onto the frozen face on his chest.

Spark ran around the other side of the house. A fence blocked her path to the neighbor's yard, so she continued to race along the wall. In a blinding flash, the security light flicked on, burning so bright it felt like daytime. The grass went from a dark sea to brilliant green. And in the middle of it, casting a long shadow, stood that skinny little squirrel again. He saw Spark approaching and raised onto his hind legs. His tail pointed out like a furry little spear. This squirrel had at last discovered his bravery. He was ready to fight.

Until, that is, he saw the monster behind Spark. He let out a squeal and darted into the bushes.

Spark ran faster, her feet splashing. *Psssh-psssh-psssh-psssh.* Thanks to the light, she could see the purple yarn, still tied to Loretta's window and flapping in the wind, dangling all the way to the lawn. She grabbed it, yanked it tight, and began to climb up the side of the house. Her paws were soaked, and they oozed water every time she squeezed the string.

She felt a shudder through the aluminum siding. To her right, Jakmal skittered across the wall like a spider, his pincer scraping a groove in its wake. Strangely, the human half of his body twisted so that it stretched out parallel to the ground, while the monstrous part of him clung to the side like an insect.

Spark felt a tug on the string. Above, Sir Reginald pulled the yarn, his leg planted against the window frame for leverage. Each time her foot slipped on the wet surface, she imagined the pincer seizing her at her waist, tearing her away from the string, from everything she knew. As she jammed herself into the open window, Sir Reginald wrapped his thick arms around her neck and tried to pull her through. An ice-cold hand gripped her ankle but then fell away as the two bears tumbled from the windowsill. Heavy with rainwater, she splatted on the floor.

Behind her, Loretta stirred under the covers. Spark motioned for Sir Reginald to help her stand. There was no time for that. The old bear dragged her under the bed, leaving a wet streak. Moments later, Loretta's bare feet planted on the floor a few inches away. The girl groggily walked over to the window and closed it. As she turned away, her toe splashed in the puddle that Spark left behind.

"Ugh," she groaned.

Loretta went to the camera and pressed the rewind button. She stared at the viewfinder as it cycled through the past few hours. With the night vision switched on, the screen created a green aura, like some otherworldly fire. When the video reached the beginning without showing anything, Loretta let out a long sigh. She leaned on the tripod and considered her next move. Then she zipped open a bag on her desk, pulled out a fresh battery, and swapped out the old one. She pressed the record button.

Spark hoped that she would call it a night then. But her dusa could not help herself. Completely unaware of the danger she was in, Loretta ran her fingers along the wall where the portal had appeared. In the corner, she crouched and tapped the little grate where hot air rose during the winter. Spark could hardly contain herself. She wanted to run to her friend and pull her away before another portal opened around her and swallowed her like a whale's mouth.

Sir Reginald tightened his grip on her. "Don't," he whispered.

After what felt like an eternity, Loretta returned to the bed. She flopped on top of the comforter and fell asleep almost instantly.

The rain lightened from a deafening roar to a gentle tapping.

Trembling, Spark kept her eyes on the window. Sir Reginald still held her by the neck. The two bears leaned into each other, not saying a word, watching for trouble until the sun rose.

SIXTEEN

Spark tried to think of a happier time.

At first, the images collapsed on one another, tumbling and spinning. She remembered Loretta crying, Loretta hiding under her bed with Spark at her side, Loretta shivering with fever and wiping her nose on Spark's fur. She remembered a late-summer afternoon, when Loretta carried her outside to show her the bright colors of Dad's garden—red tomatoes, orange pumpkins, yellow sunflowers. Every day, the world offered some new wonder, some unexpected delight.

Sir Reginald often scolded her for daydreaming like this, and yet she needed it more and more these days, with so much slipping away.

Spark finally settled on a memory: a family outing to the movies. Loretta must have been five at the time, Matthew six. Dad's hair was darker then. Mom's was longer.

The night started at the hospital, where Matthew often stayed for stretches at a time. This latest visit involved complications from another surgery. Loretta, too young to understand what was going on, dragged Spark along for the ride. She played with the bear in the corner of the room on the shiny floor that smelled like bleach, while the doctors and nurses whispered to Mom and Dad.

Spark did not like this place. Too cold, too bright, with odd noises pinging and buzzing, hushed voices, occasional crying and coughing from faraway rooms. Even with Matthew's toys strewn about—including Sir Reginald, of course—the place felt fake somehow, an unfinished dollhouse for humans. And yet Mom and Dad did everything they could to make it better, to make it all seem like a game. To make it seem normal.

On this particular night, Mom and Dad decided to do something completely different.

"We're sneaking out of here," Dad said as soon as the doctor left the room. Behind him, Mom chuckled. Loretta stopped and listened.

"What do you mean?" Matthew asked.

"*Clash of the Titans*," Dad said.

"What?"

"The original," Mom said. "They're showing it at the Forum."

"But what about . . ." Matthew looked around, lowered his voice. "What about the doctors?"

"We got a plan," Dad said. "We're bustin' out."

Spark understood then that Mom and Dad were children once, not so long ago. They could still be like children when they needed to.

The next few minutes were a blur of whispering and giggling and shushing. Mom put pillows under Matthew's covers to make it look like he was still underneath. She dressed him in his jeans and a hoodie while Dad kept watch at the door. They were about to leave when Loretta, holding Spark by the paw, started to cry.

"Shhhh!" Mom said. "Sweetie, we need you to be quiet, okay?"

"Sir Reginald wants to go with us!" Loretta sobbed.

"We have to go now."

"It's okay, Mom," Matthew said. "I'll bring him."

The four humans, with two bears in tow, slinked through the corridors, avoiding the orderlies and the nurses. They planned to sneak out the hospital's rear entrance, which meant passing through a long hallway. At every intersection, Dad would crouch to the floor and check both directions before waving them on. Loretta laughed so hard through it all that she could barely breathe. Matthew belly-crawled past the cafeteria like a ninja.

When they reached the exit, Dad ordered them to wait while he ran across the parking lot to the SUV.

"I don't want the cameras to see us!" he said.

A few seconds later, the car squealed to a stop right in front of them. To save time, Dad opened the rear door, and they all climbed into the back before the car sped away. As they settled into their seats, Dad took the exit to the highway, while James Brown's "Get Up Offa That Thing" blasted on the radio. Mom clapped along, and Loretta bounced Spark on her knee. Still dazed, Matthew watched the streetlamps as they zoomed overhead.

With their hearts still thumping, they entered the cinema lobby, where the buttery smell of popcorn hung like a cloud over everything. Parts of the floor were sticky with spilled soda. The teenage girl at the booth made a joke about how they would need to buy tickets for the teddy bears. She pointed them toward the theater, and they took their seats in the very front row, the only place that could fit all of them together.

Spark rested in Loretta's lap while the opening credits climbed the screen. The darkness, the flashing, the noises, the music, the other people—all of it made Spark panic. Though she could handle the small television screen at home, the images here towered like giants over her. This theater made it impossible to protect her dusa. But then she saw Sir Reginald, leaning on the armrest beside her. He winked. It meant that they were safe, that everything would be okay.

The children laughed at the funny parts, like when the hero Perseus found a mechanical owl. They gasped when the giant scorpions attacked. They gazed in silence when Perseus flew on a winged horse. In the final scene, Perseus battled a giant fish-like monster, the Kraken. The entire time, Loretta hid her face behind Spark's head. When the hero defeated the monster, she shook Spark like a cheerleader's pom-pom.

If Loretta and Matthew somehow possessed some special power, perhaps it all began here.

On the ride home, the family recapped the night's events. Mom said she liked Perseus the most. "He had nice hair," she said.

"Well, I liked the girl!" Dad said.

"Fine, you can like the girl."

Matthew said that the Medusa monster was his favorite. Loretta liked the owl.

"Dad," Matthew said, "are we gonna get in trouble?"

"No, big guy."

"Everything's fine," Mom said. And then she looked at Dad, and he looked at her. In the darkness, she rested her hand on his and squeezed it until her knuckles turned white. The children did not notice—they were too busy impersonating the various creatures and goblins from the movie, trying to scare each other.

Later that night, long after everyone went to bed, Sir Reginald crept into Loretta's room and whispered Spark's name. She peeled herself away from Loretta's chest and crawled to the edge of the bed.

"Are you all right?" the old bear asked.

"Yes. What is it?"

He seemed lost in thought. "You know they planned all of that, right? Mom and Dad. The doctors said Matthew could go home, but Mom and Dad asked if they could pretend to sneak him out."

"Why?" Spark asked.

"Because Matthew needed it. They all needed to feel free for a little while."

Spark could hardly recognize it in him, but the grizzled old bear was happy. So happy he could burst. He had to share it with someone.

"Well," he said, "back to our watch."

"Of course. Good night, Sir."

"Good night, Hotshot."

Spark held that memory close, like some tiny ember that could blink out in the slightest breeze. Those days were gone. Everything they had built here hung by a thread. And any minute now, the thread could break.

SEVENTEEN

The morning after Jakmal attacked, the family prepared their things for another search. It was Monday, and this break in their usual routine felt alien to Spark. This time, they would gather with their neighbors and patrol the wooded area between the town and the highway, just like they did when looking for Sofia a few days before.

While the two bears remained hidden under the bed, Loretta checked the camera again and found nothing. She put on her hiking boots, a raggedy pair of jeans, and a raincoat. She looked like a robot. No expression on her face, just a blank stare and a clenched jaw.

Downstairs, Spark could hear the parents talking at the table. At one point, Dad went outside and shouted something to Mom. Judging from the tone of his voice, he must have seen the damage to the car. Mom gasped when she saw it. "Oh my God!"

"Now they see it," Spark said. "Now they know something's wrong in this house."

"Maybe," Sir Reginald said. It meant no.

Loretta joined her parents outside, right in the middle of Dad's speech about how his insurance company might raise his rates. It was the kind of adult gibberish he was good at. Mom told him that there was nothing they could do. "Let's just take the SUV."

"He's not in the woods," Loretta said.

"Who's not in the woods, sweetie?"

"Matthew."

"Where is he, then?" Dad asked.

"He's . . ."

Oh no, Spark thought. *If they start poking around the house, it'll only make things worse.*

"Look," Loretta said, "something weird is going on around here, okay? Like, maybe we should search around here some more."

"Yesterday you told us he went looking for Sofia," Dad said.

"He did! Er, he was *going* to. But, I don't know, I think there's something here at the house that we need to look at."

"Honey," Mom said, "let's rule out the woods first, okay? You remember that boy last year, what was his name?"

"Zimmerman," Dad said.

"That's right, Joey Zimmerman. He crashed his bike into a tree, knocked himself out, and they found him wandering around the woods a few hours later."

Loretta said nothing. She had been trained her entire life to stop believing in fairy tales, and now she had to ignore all the evidence that was right in front of her.

"When we come back later, we'll go through everything, okay?" Mom said.

"It's not up for debate, Loretta," Dad said.

Mom glared at him. "Derek."

"It's not."

"Fine," Loretta said, cutting off the conversation before things got worse. What choice did she have?

The family grabbed their things, piled into the SUV, and drove off.

With her belly and feet swollen with rainwater, Spark could hardly move. Sir Reginald led her to the basement, holding her arm as she doddered with each step. On the way, Spark sniffed for the scratcher.

"He's gone for now," Sir Reginald said.

In the basement, Sir Reginald found a bucket with a plastic strainer that could wring out a mop. He helped Spark get inside and then pulled the lever as hard as he could. The device flattened her against the grille, forcing the water to dribble out. He did this a few more times until a full inch of water sat at the bottom of the bucket.

He pointed to one of the nearby machines: a white metal box with a big door and several dials on top. Though Spark had seen the bucket in the kitchen before, she didn't know what these machines did.

"Get in," Sir Reginald said.

"What is that?"

"It will dry you off. You'll feel better."

"I'm fine."

"If you do not get dry, you will smell like mildew. We cannot risk having Loretta put you in the attic because you stink."

The threat of the attic was enough to make Spark get inside.

Sir Reginald dropped in a tiny white tissue that smelled like flowers. He found a weathered sneaker nearby and tossed it into the dryer with her.

"It will soften you up," he said. "Be grateful I am not putting you in the washing machine."

He closed the door. She heard him turning the dials. Then the tiny chamber began to tumble, knocking her over. A blast of heat warmed her fur. The machine spun relentlessly, dropping the shoe on top of her again and again.

"Is it supposed to do this?" she shouted.

"Yes! It will dry you more quickly!"

Each time the heel of the sneaker landed on her, she got angrier and angrier about what had happened the night before. The monster set a trap for them. Or he tested them. Either way, he wanted to get rid of the bears so that he could take Loretta.

Eventually, the dryer beeped and the chamber slowed to a halt. Sir Reginald opened the door. Though dizzy, Spark felt light again, fluffy. She kicked the shoe away.

"I need to show you something," Sir Reginald said.

The living room window provided the best view of the damaged car, a cherry-red sedan that Mom bought when she finished grad school a couple of years earlier. A deep crack had formed in the center of the windshield, stretching out into a spider web from end to end. The hood bent inward, crumpled beyond repair. And on top of the car, strategically placed, lay an enormous tree branch, its wet leaves flattened against the metal.

"This Jakmal is smart," Sir Reginald said. "He knows how humans think."

"That branch is too small to do all that damage!" Spark said.

"A falling branch is still more likely than a monster from another dimension."

"But maybe Mom and Dad can help us."

"No. They do not believe in us anymore."

"I know it's against the rules," Spark said, "but what if—"

"No."

"I didn't finish my question!"

"I know what you are going to ask. You want to talk to them. It does not work like that."

"This is different," she said.

"We are not helping anyone if we do that," he said.

He told her a story she had heard many times. Sir Reginald knew of a bear named Freddy who belonged to one of Dad's classmates many years earlier. One night, Freddy's dusa wanted to sneak out of the house by sliding down the rain spout. When Freddy tried to warn him not to do it, the boy thought his bear was possessed. Panicking, he threw Freddy out the window. And then the boy had to go to a therapist, who eventually convinced him that he had imagined the entire thing. Meanwhile, Freddy disappeared.

For all they knew, Jakmal was trying to trick them into speaking to Mom and Dad.

"We are on our own," Sir Reginald said. He climbed down from the windowsill, leaving Spark to stare at the wreckage of the car.

"Come on," he said. "It is our turn to set a trap."

EIGHTEEN

Spark and Sir Reginald started in the basement, searching for anything they could use as a weapon. However, the tools they wanted most were too heavy to lift. It would take both of them to carry the axe to Loretta's room, and even then, they would have no way to swing it at the monster. The tools in the garage posed the same problem. Spark wanted the sledgehammer, but rigging it so it would fall on the monster would take too long. They debated dragging the nail gun upstairs. It would do little damage and would most likely make Jakmal even angrier. Still, a well-placed shot could disable the scratcher. They decided to bring it with them.

A far better weapon: the circular saw with a portable battery. If they could score a direct hit, it would make Jakmal scream, maybe even shear off one of his skinny insect legs. They decided to hide both power tools in the shoeboxes under Loretta's bed. Dad had not used them in a while, so hopefully he would not notice their absence.

After lugging the equipment to the bedroom, they dug

through Loretta's cabinets and drawers searching for anything sharp enough to pierce Jakmal's scales.

Zed shouted to them from the bookshelf. "Sir Reginald! It's good to see you!"

"Where were you last night?" Sir Reginald said. "Why didn't you help us?"

"I was here! Right here."

"Stay there, Zed," Spark said, sifting through the items on the floor of the closet. She glanced at Sir Reginald and shrugged. This was not the time to start lecturing people on their duties. Zed never swore an oath like they did.

"What are you doing?" the monkey asked.

"I'm trying to figure out which weapon to give you," she said. "For when the monster comes back."

"He's coming back?" Zed squeezed into a ball and shivered.

Sir Reginald ignored him. "Find anything?"

Spark wrenched a curling iron from underneath a pile of shoes. "This gets really hot," she said. "What did *you* find?"

"I like *this*," he said, brandishing a small pair of scissors like a dagger.

A vehicle pulled into the driveway—Dad's SUV. "Quick, quick," Spark said, motioning to the others. With no time to hide the scissors, Sir Reginald dropped them into an open drawer. She led him to the linen closet. Downstairs, the family entered the kitchen. Spark heard them unzipping their coats. Someone dragged a chair from the table and flopped onto it, exhausted.

"You cannot go down there," Sir Reginald said, reading her mind. "Wait in Loretta's room like we said."

"I'll see you tonight," she said, shutting the door on him.

Spark tiptoed to the staircase, where she peeked through the bars of the railing into the kitchen. There, Mom and Loretta sat at the table facing each other. The microwave beeped. Dad walked over with three mugs of hot chocolate piping with steam. He set the cups on the table and sat in a chair.

No one spoke. Their jackets glistened with rainwater. Mud and grass caked their boots. Mom wore a bandage on her hand—probably a cut from a branch or a thorn. She tried to tie her tangled hair into a bun several times before quitting and letting it dangle.

"Every time we look for him, we rule out another place," Dad said. "That's how we—"

Mom stood, scraping her chair along the tiles. She walked outside without closing the door behind her. A chilling silence descended on the kitchen. Loretta wrapped her hands around her cup for warmth.

"Are you okay?" Dad asked.

"Yes," she lied.

Loretta excused herself. Dad did not ask her why, nor did he tell her to remove her muddy boots before marching across the carpet. Instead, he ran his hands over his growing beard.

Spark returned to her spot on the bed before Loretta arrived. The girl was so tired that she sloughed off the wet jacket, kicked away her boots, and face-planted onto the comforter. She smelled like a puddle. Spark noticed dirt under Loretta's fingernails and grass stains on her pants.

After a few minutes of lying still, Loretta shimmied to the edge of the mattress and reached into the pocket of her coat. She pulled out her phone and scrolled through the numbers until she found the one she wanted. She tapped it with her thumb, pressed the phone to her ear, and waited.

"Hey," came a voice on the other end. It was Darcy.

"Hey."

"Are you okay?" Darcy asked.

"Yeah. Here's the thing. Um . . . we're going to do this movie. Okay?"

Dead silence on the other end.

"Can you still make it?" Loretta added.

"I thought you didn't want to."

"I changed my mind. Matthew—"

She cupped her hand over her mouth and choked on a sob.

"Matthew asked me to do it," she finally said. "Before he . . . before he left."

"You still think he's out looking for Sofia?"

Loretta sat upright in her bed and stared at the claw mark on the wall.

"I know this is crazy," Loretta said, "but something weird is going on around here. I tried to tell my parents. But it's only gonna stress them out."

"Okay," Darcy said.

"Matthew said something to me, about Sofia. That she was afraid of something, something coming to get her. And then she disappeared. But not before making Matthew swear that he'd finish the movie. And now *he's* gone."

Darcy let out a long "Ummmmm."

"I've been looking around for clues," Loretta said. "But maybe there's a clue *in the movie*. Like, if we make it, this'll all make sense." She slapped her palm on her forehead. It sounded so stupid when she said it out loud.

"But how—" Darcy stopped. Because she was a good friend, she decided not to press Loretta on this. "What about the others?"

The others, Spark thought. Claire and Jisha.

"I wanted to check with you first," Loretta said. "They're gonna say yes if you do. They better!"

"We're gonna do it, I swear. If you want us to do it, we'll do it."

They spoke for a little while longer. Darcy kept saying that they could wait. Loretta told her again and again, more forcefully each time, that they were making the movie.

"I'm sick of it," Loretta said. "I'm sick of everyone asking me if I'm okay. No matter how many times I say it, no one believes me."

"But you're *not* okay," Darcy said.

Loretta sat still for a moment. Her nose scrunched as she tried to keep herself from crying. "Fine. I'm not. We're doing this anyway, or I'm gonna be even worse."

Darcy let out a little laugh. "They're gonna find him, Lor. Sofia, too. I know it."

After she said goodbye, Loretta rocked back and forth. Though Spark could not read her thoughts, she did not have to. The girl was so close to figuring it all out. Loretta could sense the strange powers swirling around her, pushing and pulling at her, though she could not speak of them. Not yet.

Quietly, Spark turned to the wall, where the claw mark still slashed through one of the posters. It mocked her. This monster wanted a fight. And unlike her, he wasn't afraid.

NINETEEN

After a quick dinner of Chinese takeout, Mom and Dad dropped Loretta off at Grandma's house. She would spend the night there while her parents took care of a few things. First on their list: an awkward phone call with the detective, which they did not want Loretta to hear. Spark listened from the top of the stairs while Mom and Dad got the latest update from the police. The detective, his voice tinny on the speaker, explained that they were still combing through hours of footage from security cameras around the neighborhood. Tomorrow, they would search the riverbank. And they would interview more people at the school to see what they knew.

"Hold on, hold on," Dad said. "My son and the Lopez girl—are they connected or not?"

The detective paused. "We're questioning Mr. Lopez, and we are trying to get in touch with Sofia's mother as well—"

"But are they connected? You've gotta know something."

Mom tried to intervene. "We passed out flyers for Sofia a few days ago. All of us. The whole town was doing it. Was there anyone suspicious there? Someone who wasn't supposed to be there?"

Neither parent had slept much since Matthew disappeared, and it showed. They were grasping for clues. Two vanished children in less than a week would do that.

When the detective said for the third time that they were doing everything they could, Dad pounded his fist on the table.

"Did they run away or they were kidnapped?" he said. "Can you at least tell us that?"

The detective cleared his throat.

"Can you?" Dad said.

"We can't say yet."

Dad propped his elbows on the table and buried his face in his hands.

"Derek," Mom said. Spark imagined her placing her hand on his arm.

"There is one thing we could try," the detective said. He told them that he had called one of his friends, a cop who worked downtown. The cop put together a collection of mug shots. Maybe Mom and Dad could go through them, see if they recognized anyone who may have been snooping around the neighborhood. "It's a long shot," the detective said, "but at least you'll be doing something. You'll be ruling out another possibility, ya know what I mean?"

They agreed right away. After ending the call, they put on their coats, grabbed the car keys, and switched off the lights. They argued a little over the fastest way to get downtown—Dad always knew some shortcut, but Mom said that this was not the time to show off.

"Wait," Mom said. "Are we really going to let Loretta do this movie thing tomorrow?"

Dad sighed. "I don't know."

Loretta had asked about it at dinner that night. Mom and Dad had both said "We'll see" at the same time.

Mom and Dad continued to debate it in the driveway. Spark ran to Loretta's bedroom window, where she continued to listen.

"Might be good for her," Mom said.

"I guess so, sure," Dad grumbled.

"You guess so." Mom opened her side of the car and got in. The seatbelt alarm went *bong-bong-bong-bong*.

"You're right," Dad said. "It'll keep her mind off this stuff for a few hours."

Dad hopped in and started the car. They sped off. Spark sat by the window for a while. Thinking.

When she was finished, she raced to the basement, where she found Sir Reginald rummaging through Dad's toolbox searching for more weapons.

"What is it?" he asked, wielding a screwdriver.

"I'm calling a juro," Spark said.

Calling a juro was the distress signal, the panic button, the call to arms for all members of the League of Ursus. It was what they feared and what they lived for: a blood oath between faithful bears to fight evil. None could refuse.

"What are you talking about?" Sir Reginald said.

"We're not on our own," she said. "The other bears will help. Ozzie and Lulu. Rana, too." She told him about the movie. Loretta planned to make it after all, and Mom and Dad had agreed. The others would arrive tomorrow, on the first day of their spring break. Matthew had hoped to spend the holiday editing the footage with Sofia and adding special effects on his computer.

Sir Reginald dropped the screwdriver. "Oh, no."

"What is it?"

"This is what the monster wants. Do you not see it? All those children in one place. He could take them all."

Spark wondered if Jakmal had planned this somehow. Perhaps he hoped to wipe out all the bears at once, leaving the entire neighborhood defenseless.

"The bears will be here, too," she said. "Maybe they already saw our signal."

Sir Reginald still did not trust these other bears. They were too soft, he always said. "They do not know this house."

"We can't do this on our own," Spark said. "And we can't wait for the Grand Sleuth to send help. Loretta's my dusa. This is my call to make."

"*Your* call?"

"Yes. The bear who is actively protecting a dusa takes command of a juro."

"I am protecting my . . ." He stopped when he realized that it was too late for that. "But this . . . this is a technicality!"

"It sure is," Spark said.

Sir Reginald put his paws on his hips. For the briefest of moments, he seemed almost proud of her for beating him at his own game.

"I can still offer advice," he said.

"I'll need it."

"Very well," Sir Reginald said. "I want you to consider all your options. So consider this: if we can guard this house for a few more nights, this monster might go away. We will not need to risk everything—"

"He won't stop until he takes her. And we're barely guarding the house as it is."

"But it must have crossed your mind. We might be better off breaking Loretta's camera. Or doing anything we can to stop those children from coming here."

Spark squeezed her paw into a stubby little fist. It had been a long few days, poisoned with anger and fear. She was tired of it. Tired of being afraid.

"No," Spark said. "I understand what you're saying. But we have to make a stand now."

Sir Reginald reached for the screwdriver again. "Very well," he said. "Bears serve."

"I guess this is how I'll earn a sword like yours."

Sir Reginald nodded. "The Grand Sleuth will be proud."

Spark imagined what it would be like, a long time from now, when the high council of the League called on her. She would be ready. She would go where she was needed.

"We have less than a day," she said. "Let's get moving."

Sir Reginald planted the handle of the screwdriver on the floor as if wielding a spear.

If Jakmal decided to probe their defenses again, they would make him regret it.

TWENTY

With the house to themselves, and Loretta safe at Grandma's, Spark and Sir Reginald gathered their supplies, laid their traps, mapped out all possible escape routes. There was simply not enough time to prepare. Then again, all the time in the world may not have been enough.

In the basement, surrounded by their tools of war, Spark and Sir Reginald agreed on a strategy. First, they would lure Jakmal out of hiding. They could not detect his scent in either the basement or the attic, leaving Loretta's room as the most likely location of his next attack. But the room was too small for a fight. In close quarters, Jakmal enjoyed the advantage. One swipe of his tail could rip the bears apart. Rather than fight him directly, they would keep the portal open, the same way Sir Reginald had in his first encounter with the monster. An obstacle—even one as thin as an electrical cord—could prevent the gateway from closing. If it worked out like last time, the portal would shift and carry them into the attic, where a few surprises awaited. In a larger area, the bears would have space to run. They could set traps and hide behind barricades. They could open fire.

"That's not the only reason you want to keep the portal open, is it?" Spark asked.

Sir Reginald looked at her.

"You want to see if Matthew is still in there," she said. "You want a rescue mission."

Sir Reginald turned away from her. "I cannot ask you to do that. I cannot ask all of you to go into the portal. It's too risky."

"If we can defeat this monster, and hold the portal open, then it's worth a shot."

"No," he said. "The portal is unstable. Even after we destroy the scratcher, the doorway will take some time before it finally collapses. And when that happens, you will want to be as far away from it as you can get."

"What do you suggest then?"

"If we go into the rift, we will need to be quick about it. Perhaps I can sneak into the portal once it opens."

Spark snorted out a little laugh. "Now who's being risky?"

"I am risking myself!"

She could not blame him for this. But she needed to take control of the situation. Otherwise, they would get stuck debating things, and by the time they finished, the monster would have made off with another child.

"I need everyone focused on defeating this monster," Spark said. "If the opportunity arises to go into the portal, I'll give the order. But you said so yourself: destroying the scratcher is the top priority. We can't screw this up. We can't lose *both* of them."

"What would you do if you were me?" he asked.

"I would follow the code. We protect the living, not the dead."

Though it sounded true, it was a lie. If Loretta were trapped in the portal, Spark would dive right in to find her. Nothing else would matter.

Sir Reginald glared at her. He had taught her everything, and now she spoke to him as if he were a cub.

"I'm sorry," she said, hugging him. "I'm sorry, I didn't mean it like that. We have to protect Loretta. I need you to help me, or we'll lose everything. Please."

"You're right, Hotshot. I will wait for you to give the order."

They spent the night fortifying the attic, building ramparts and siege walls. They removed some of the floorboards to create tiny trenches. They embedded dozens of nails into a piece of plywood and laid it flat, a minefield for Jakmal to cross if he dared. On the ceiling, they fastened several rows of razor blades, which would prevent him from scaling the walls. They hauled more equipment from the basement and the garage. Heavy things, like dumbbells, cinderblocks, a crowbar. And as much rope and fishing wire as they could find.

They paused only when Mom and Dad returned from the police station. Luckily, the parents went right to bed and fell asleep, having run themselves ragged for three days. Once Dad started snoring, the bears resumed their work.

The next thing they needed was armor. For this, Spark fashioned a set of vests by cutting apart a leather jacket that Dad hadn't worn since college. Each vest could fit over the body of a teddy bear. To add a little flavor, she spiked them with sewing needles and razors. Out of the leather and fabric that remained she created cuffs for the elbows and ankles, attaching sharp points to these as well. If the monster grabbed her by the tail, she could drive a sharpened elbow into his claw. If the monster knocked her over, she could still kick him with the spurs on her heels. Every part of her became a weapon.

"I like it," Sir Reginald said.

And finally, the artillery. At the far end of the attic they arranged four white plastic pipes, all aimed at the spot where Jakmal would emerge. Inside each, a rocket from the Fourth of July waited for its fuse to be lit. Though they would do little damage, the fireworks might convince the monster that even more dangerous weapons awaited.

To this artillery, Sir Reginald added a wrist-rocket slingshot. It was the same one that Dad confiscated from Matthew a couple of years earlier, after the boy accidentally shot out a headlight on the family car. But before he set the slingshot beside the other weapons, Sir Reginald cradled it as if it were his own.

"What's wrong?" Spark asked.

"I know why Dad couldn't throw this away," he said. "He owned one himself when he was Matthew's age. When he was my dusa."

Sir Reginald told her then about Dad many years before, when his name was Derek, and he looked just like Matthew. But unlike his son, Derek did not have the same ability to conjure stories in his mind. He didn't have a dream journal or a movie poster collection. Instead, he rallied the other neighborhood kids to create all sorts of mischief that the adults tolerated— at least for a while. Ringing on doorbells and running away, accidentally denting the cars on the block with baseballs, building a dam in the creek until it overflowed and flooded Mrs. Mitchell's flower bed. One summer, Derek broke his leg trying to climb a tree. He needed to recover in bed for a while. Sir Reginald sat with him while he watched the same four movies for days on end. Including *Clash of the Titans*, of course.

The following Christmas, Derek cleaned his room, on orders from his father. He placed Sir Reginald in his parents' attic, where the bear stayed for years. "It wasn't so bad," the bear said. After all, he had seen Derek safely through childhood, which is what the League of Ursus was meant to do. There he stayed for a long time. Season after season passed, snow then spring, sunshine then fall. More objects piled into the tiny space. Though isolated, Sir Reginald still thought of himself as responsible for watching over the house.

Until one day, a young man entered—tall, wearing glasses and a college sweatshirt. After a few seconds, Sir Reginald recognized the man as Derek, all grown up. And behind him was a woman he called Julie, who would one day become Mom. She waddled along with an enormous belly.

"Oh, here he is!" Derek said, plucking Sir Reginald from the pile.

"That is so cute," Julie said, grinning. "Ugh, he's all dusty."

Derek patted Sir Reginald so that the dust motes exploded from his fur.

"Derek!"

"What?" he said, laughing.

Julie insisted that Sir Reginald pay a visit to the washing

machine. Upon hearing this, Spark recalled her own experience in the dryer.

"What was it like?" she asked.

"I did not care for it."

Still, the spin cycle was worth it. Sir Reginald soon became Matthew's best friend. He stuck with the boy through all the trips to the hospital, all the years of physical therapy, all the late nights crying because someone at school made fun of him. Matthew learned to be kinder than his own parents. He listened more. He laughed and sang more. And then, when Loretta came along, so too did another bear. With each passing day, the four humans (and two bears) became stronger together. They became a family. Not merely something they promised to protect, but something worth protecting. Something that could slip away so easily, which is what made it so precious.

"We are lucky to have children this special," Sir Reginald said.

Before Spark could ask more questions, Sir Reginald went about inspecting the firecrackers once more. "We need a real lighter for the fuses instead of these matches," he said. "We cannot take any chances."

He needed to go on planning, like a good bear. Spark let him do it. As the sun began to rise, they covered the barricades with bedsheets and moved the artillery range behind the piano. Once again, they parted ways in the hall.

Another long day still lay ahead. They needed to stay sharp. They needed to hang on until help arrived.

TWENTY-ONE

Grandma's giant red Cadillac pulled into the driveway around seven in the morning. Spark recognized the purr of the engine. Loretta hopped out, said goodbye, and ran inside the house. Hearing her voice was a huge relief for Spark. Sitting in her spot between the pillows, she allowed herself a few moments of believing that maybe they had scared this monster away for good. But then she remembered the growing battlefield in the attic above her. On this day, the last before spring break, school would be dismissed at noon, and the young filmmakers would arrive around six in the evening. This gave the bears only a few hours for final preparations. Every second counted.

While Loretta ate breakfast in the kitchen, Spark could not resist the urge to see her. She jumped from the bed and peeked into the hall. As she crossed the threshold of the door, Sir Reginald appeared right in front of her. She yelped in surprise.

"It's too early!" she whispered. "Get back in your closet!"

"We have a problem. Dad knows something's missing from the basement."

Sir Reginald cupped his paw to his ear. On the first floor, Dad stomped around shouting. "You sure you didn't take it for your movie?"

"No, Dad," Loretta said. "Why would I need that?"

"What are they looking for?" Spark asked. Sir Reginald shushed her.

"Well, *somebody's* been moving things around," Dad said.

"What do you need it for anyway?"

"I need it to open the trunk. Before the tow truck gets here."

Spark put it together in her mind: the damaged car still sat in the driveway. With the trunk caved in, the key would not work. Dad needed something to jimmy it open. Her mind raced through all of the tools they had stolen from the basement.

"Did you check the garage?" Mom asked him.

"Yes!"

"Do we keep tools in the attic?"

"Well, not anymore, but . . ."

"Okay, what about this?"

"It's a Phillips-head," Dad said. "I need a flat-head."

Spark and Sir Reginald said the word at the same time: "Screwdriver."

Dad approached the staircase.

"I have an idea," Spark said. She ran to the stairs that led to the attic, with Sir Reginald loping behind her. At the top step, Spark climbed onto Sir Reginald's shoulders and turned the knob. The two of them nearly tumbled over as the door swung open. They shut it quietly. Dad was only a few seconds behind them.

Spark ran to the artillery, where she flipped the sheet away to look for the screwdriver. "Where is it? Where is it?"

"Here!" Sir Reginald said, holding it out like a sword. She swiped it from him.

"Grab that fishing line over there," she said. He held the spool. Spark took the end and walked over to the window. She opened it.

"No," he said.

"*Yes*. Now don't let go."

Before he could argue, she dropped out the window and rappelled along the side of the building with the screwdriver tucked under her arm. Below her, the side door of the house drew closer. She landed on the knob and turned it, not caring how much noise she made. When it creaked open, she could see all the way down the steps into the basement. At the foot of the stairs was Dad's workbench.

"Hurry!" Sir Reginald shouted. "He's almost here!"

She needed to gain her footing. "Lower me more!"

When she reached the floor, she heaved the screwdriver down the steps. It hit the top of the desk with an enormous clatter before rolling off and bouncing on the floor.

"What was that?" Mom asked.

Spark stepped outside. "Up!" she said.

Sir Reginald pulled the line. As Spark passed the knob, she tried to grab it, only to have the metal slip from her paw. Once she was above the frame, she heard Mom grumble about the door being left open.

Halfway to the top, the line suddenly stopped. She tugged on it. Nothing happened. "Up!" she said. Still nothing. So she climbed, one arm over another, until she reached the attic window. There, she heard Dad's footsteps right outside the door.

Spark made it halfway in when she saw Sir Reginald, hiding in the corner, still holding the line. He put his paw to his mouth to tell her to be quiet.

The door opened.

"Derek!" Mom shouted. "Derek, I found it!"

"What? Where?"

"In the basement!"

"The *base*ment?"

After what seemed like an eternity, Dad shut the door and trudged down the stairs. Sir Reginald emerged from his hiding spot and helped Spark wriggle inside. They tried to listen.

"You left it on the side of the desk," Mom said. "It fell and hit the floor."

Judging from the way their voices traveled, Mom and Dad met in the living room, where she handed him the screwdriver.

"Where was it?" he asked.

"The desk! I told you!"

"There's no way it was there!"

"Derek, that's where I found it!"

Their voices erupted in an argument. Dad stamped his foot when he yelled at her, telling her to stay away from his things in the basement. Mom told him that it wasn't her fault he didn't know where he left his tools.

They stopped when Loretta stood quickly, knocking her chair over. She raced to her room and locked herself inside. Instead of apologizing, Mom and Dad walked away from each other, he to the driveway, she to the den.

Spark imagined Loretta hiding under her covers, sniffling. Spark was not there for her. A lead weight sank into her stomach. Before all this, Loretta would have made some smart aleck joke.

"Hey, Dad," she'd say. "This is like that time you asked me where your glasses were, and they were on your face."

Then Mom would have joined in. "You'd forget your own butt if it wasn't screwed on."

"Well, then I'm glad it's screwed on," Dad would reply. "Because then I'd go to work with no butt. Okay?"

It was a nice thought. Spark wondered if the family would ever laugh like that again.

"They were never like this before," Sir Reginald said.

"That's why we're doing this," Spark said.

TWENTY-TWO

Darcy arrived first. Spark listened from the bedroom as Loretta greeted her. Jisha arrived soon after. Both of them marveled at the set Loretta had created in the living room and the den. They ogled the digital camera. There was an awkwardness to it all, as if Jisha and Darcy were acting out a script that someone had written for them. Loretta played along. After all, she was the one who demanded that they make this movie so they could do something normal, whatever that even meant anymore.

While waiting for Claire to arrive, the girls recapped their day at school. They each took turns impersonating their math teacher, who had threatened to give them a quiz on their first day back. Judging from the raspy voice, their teacher must have smoked a pack of cigarettes a day.

"We didn't have cell phones in my day," Loretta said. "You kids have no idea. No idea!" And then she started coughing furiously, which this teacher did whenever she got upset.

At one point, Jisha went to the bathroom. Things got quiet for a moment. Spark pressed her ear to the floor to listen.

"How did it go with the search?" Darcy asked.

"Forty-two people showed up," Loretta said.

"Did you find anything?"

"Nothing."

"I'm sorry, Lor."

Darcy promised to be at the next one. When Jisha returned, Loretta changed the subject to Khaled and Jackson, the boys at school who tossed a lunch tray like a Frisbee across the cafeteria that morning. While the girls debated why they did it, and what kind of punishment they would get, the doorbell rang again. It was Claire, late as usual. She huffed and puffed as she entered, as if simply existing left her drained.

Claire apologized for being late. "My mom was being stupid," she said, dropping her purse onto the couch.

Darcy asked if she had heard the gossip about the boys. "Yeah," Claire said, "I was there." It was her slick way of reminding the others that she would always know things that they did not.

Loretta steered the conversation to the movie. "Let me get our actors," she said.

Loretta ran up the stairs, grabbed Spark and Zed, and carried them to the living room. She dropped them near the fireplace, next to Ozzie, Lulu, and Rana, Amazon Princess™. Spark remained still, though on the inside she was overjoyed to see them. Ozzie, the powerful polar bear. Lulu, the cunning panda. And Rana, the brave warrior and bona fide monster slayer.

"Hold on," Claire said. "Where's the black bear? From last time?"

Jisha and Darcy glared at her.

"He's missing, too," Loretta said. She cleared her throat and coughed once, which was what she did whenever she tried to keep from crying.

An awkward silence. "Oh," Claire said. "*Oh*, okay, yeah."

Jisha and Darcy looked at each other.

"Do you have your scripts?" Loretta asked. Claire said she didn't have time to print hers. Loretta told them to wait while she printed another.

As soon as Loretta left, Claire turned to the others. "Is she for real? Like, are we really doing this?"

"Of course we are," Darcy said.

"Didn't she tell you?" Jisha asked.

"Well, yeah, but . . . I didn't think she was serious."

"She's always serious about this stuff," Jisha said.

"My mom told me to come over," Claire said. "Ya know, to check on her." She leaned in and whispered: "My mom saw Loretta's mom at the supermarket talking with some of the women who work there, and she was crying like crazy, and they couldn't get her to stop."

"Wouldn't you be?" Darcy said.

"Yeah, but . . . I just think this is weird."

"My mom said Loretta might need this," Darcy said. "To like, feel connected to Matthew or something."

"Mine did, too," Jisha said.

Darcy was about to say something else when Loretta returned. Loretta must have known that they were talking about her. And yet she soldiered on.

"Let's get started," she said.

Loretta showed them the shooting schedule. All the shots were mapped out, down to the briefest scenes that would take only a few seconds of screen time. All they needed to do was follow the schedule, and they would be finished by midnight, depending on how long their pizza break lasted.

Mom and Dad graciously agreed to hang out in their bedroom to give the girls space. This worried Spark. The parents had never apologized to each other after their argument that morning. After another fruitless day of driving around the neighborhood and talking to the police, they seemed so tired, so defeated. The detective told them to take it easy, because they would only burn themselves out trying to search on their own. When Mom suggested they watch a movie in bed, Dad mumbled something about how he might doze off anyway. Mom did not respond.

Resting on the floor, Spark got her first good look at the makeshift set that Loretta had created. Behind the couch, a forest sprouted on the carpet, made of model trees taken from Dad's train set in the basement. By holding the camera very close to it, Loretta could make this tiny patch resemble a sprawling wilderness. On the kitchen floor, Loretta had placed a large cardboard box. The inside of it was painted like some kind of dungeon—the place from which the heroes would escape midway through the movie.

Loretta knelt in front of the coffee table and went through the shooting schedule while the girls sat on the couch. Meanwhile, Spark tried to get the others' attention.

"I need your help," she whispered. Ozzie and Lulu blinked in response. It was the universal sign of trust among bears when humans were around. That meant they were listening. Rana remained still, though she was close enough to hear.

"I'm calling a juro," Spark said. Ozzie clenched his jaw. Lulu's eyes darted about until she got them under control.

"A what?" Rana asked.

Spark used the words that Sir Reginald had taught her.

"In the name of the Founders, I call on all bears to be true," she said. "I pledge you my life if you lend me your sword."

A few feet away, the girls giggled at some joke Loretta made.

"You have my sword and my life," Ozzie said. "Until the final light."

"You have my sword and my life," Lulu repeated. "Until the final light."

"I heard about the symbol you painted on your house," Ozzie said. "I'm sorry I could not come sooner."

"What are you bears talking about?" Rana asked.

"There's a monster attacking this house," Spark said. "It took the boy. We're going to fight it."

"Come on. A *real* monster? Not a fake one that your friend made up in her head?"

"Yes, a real one. Maybe like the one you killed."

Rana held in a laugh. "Sure. I'll help you, little bear."

Spark wondered if she could ever giggle in the face of certain doom. Bears weren't made like that. They worried. They rarely made jokes. This Amazon did not fear death.

"What about the monkey?" Lulu whispered.

"Leave me out of this!" Zed said.

"He's a lookout," Spark said.

"No I'm not!"

"He'll scream at the first sign of trouble."

"No I won't!" Zed thought about this for a moment. "Okay, maybe I will."

"Sir Reginald is hiding upstairs," Spark said. "After this movie is finished, we'll meet him there. We'll—"

She stopped talking when Loretta walked over and grabbed her. "So, the first thing is going to be an establishing shot, with Spark in the foreground. Easy."

The girls nodded. It was time to begin.

TWENTY-THREE

Loretta took charge in a way that Spark had never seen before. If Spark did not know better, she would never have guessed that this girl had the weight of the world pressing down on her. She was indestructible. If it was true that Jakmal needed exceptional children to break his curse, then it made sense that he would seek out someone like her.

Loretta set the timer on her cell phone to make sure they stayed on schedule. To do that, they needed to complete each shot within five minutes and forty-two seconds. She gave an extra two minutes to shots that required heavy dialogue, to accommodate mistakes. Jisha was often guilty of laughing while spouting silly lines like, "Fortune favors the bold!" More than once, Claire said her lines in a voice that could only be described as bored. She did not like when Loretta told her to try again. Neither did Rana, whom Claire held like a puppet. Spark worried that the Amazon Princess might break character and put her hands on her hips or something.

They shot the movie out of order, starting with the dungeon escape scene in the kitchen. "Wait, what page are we on?" Claire asked. Loretta explained that starting the shoot here allowed them to get the difficult part out of the way and to reuse part of the set for another scene later. Though Claire did not understand, she went along with it.

Spark remembered the storyboards she saw in Matthew's room, so she knew what to expect in this scene. Still, it felt strange. At that very moment, Matthew, or Sofia, or someone else might be in a similar place, waiting for rescue. If they were still alive at all. At least Sir Reginald did not have to see this.

Without the old bear, the girls used a plush soldier toy for his role. The soldier wore an olive-green uniform and a round helmet, which made him look like the men from the World War II documentaries that Dad liked to watch. Dad had given the toy to Matthew a few years earlier, but Matthew never bonded with it, and so the soldier never came to life. Still, the soldier's noble face and square jaw worked well for his role. He merely sat there while Loretta spoke his lines in a voice that sounded suspiciously like Dad when he lectured her about cleaning her room. Spark held in a laugh while she listened.

The shoot proceeded as planned, on time. Loretta methodically shuffled the crew through the schedule, checking off each scene. Jisha insisted on using the clapperboard, which helped to keep things moving. They didn't really need it—clapperboards were used only with film cameras, not digital—but it was fun to have Jisha hold it out and say, "Scene 8, take 3!" and then snap the two sticks together.

The only thing that interfered with the schedule was the arrival of the pizza delivery guy. Dad emerged from his room to pay for it. After he left, the girls sat around eating and laughing. The greasy smell reminded Spark of the scratcher, but she remained calm.

"That guy who brought the pizza," Claire said. "Was that Jodie's older brother?"

"I think so," Jisha said.

"I heard he got kicked off the basketball team. That's why he's delivering pizzas."

When the girls asked what happened, Claire told them he had been caught drawing graffiti in the boys' bathroom. The girls did not believe that this would get someone kicked off the team—certainly not someone who was all-county the year before. Claire swore it was true.

Loretta cut the conversation short to stay on track. It was not easy—everyone was tired and full of pizza. They still needed to film the part of the movie that Sofia had added, the ending. And it was at that point that Claire asked a question that had already been answered.

"Why aren't we just doing all the scenes in order?"

Darcy shook her head and pinched the bridge of her nose.

"Because it's easier this way," Loretta said. She explained— once again—that they needed to shoot the movie out of order so they would not have to rearrange the sets. This was how real movies worked. One of the first episodes of LM^2 discussed this very topic. Jisha and Darcy seemed to get it—or at least went along with it. Claire would not budge.

"Why don't we just do the ship scene next?" Claire said. "That way, we follow right along in the script."

"Here's the thing," Loretta said. "The script helps you set up the schedule. Then you have to *follow* the schedule. Like we're doing now. I told you this."

"Yeah, but it doesn't make any sense."

"I just explained it!"

They went back and forth until Jisha held up Loretta's cell phone. "Time's up on this scene."

Claire would not let it go. Spark watched as Loretta grew more frustrated. She wanted to stand up and tell Claire to give it a rest.

"I could be doing something else tonight," Claire said.

"Yeah, you could!" Loretta said.

And then, something amazing happened. Loretta stepped forward, close enough to make Claire back away. "You promised you would do this," she said. "You walk out now, that's fine. I'll reshoot the whole thing without you."

Claire pursed her lips, unable to speak. Loretta had called her bluff.

"Okay," Claire said. "Fine."

And with that, the filmmakers continued. As the girls set up the scene, Loretta did not even mention the argument. Instead, she reset the timer and positioned the camera. The shot involved the hero and the villain—played by Spark and Ozzie—in a climactic sword fight. As the villain appears to get the upper hand and prepares to deliver the death blow, the hero unleashes her magic powers, hidden for so long, and vanquishes her foe. Loretta read the lines earnestly, perfectly, in one take. Before anyone could compliment her, Loretta hustled them along to the next scene. They had a schedule to keep!

Spark was so proud of her friend. Maybe Loretta possessed this power that Jakmal wanted. Maybe she didn't. Either way, all of this madness was making her stronger. Spark felt stronger, too. For years, she had worried about the day when Loretta would move on without her. When she would leave Spark in an attic or give her away to a thrift store, where she would wait for the Grand Sleuth to finally call her to some new mission. For the first time, none of that bothered Spark. Loretta was on her way to becoming a new person. A person who would no longer need a teddy bear. Now that Spark could see what the future looked like, it made sense. She would protect her dusa on this journey no matter where it led.

After the girls finished, they rolled out their sleeping bags and watched some reality TV show in which people in their early twenties lived in an apartment and argued over whose turn it was to take out the trash. With the screen glowing, they talked about school, about what they planned to do that summer. Spark barely heard the words. She preferred to listen to the sounds of their voices. For a while, it was nothing but giddy laughter and shrieks and whispers. They switched off the lights and kept talking late into the night.

Come on, Spark thought. *It's time to go to bed.*

Before they faded out for the night, Jisha asked Loretta what was on all of their minds. "So we shot the movie," she said. "Did you get the clues you were looking for?"

Loretta rolled onto her side, facing away from her friends. "No," she said. "Not yet. Maybe when I look at the footage tomorrow."

The digital clock on the entertainment center switched over to one in the morning.

"Did Matthew really believe all this stuff about monsters and magic and all that?" Jisha asked.

"Well, Sofia did," Loretta said. "I guess Matthew did, too."

"The movie *did* tell us something," Darcy said. "You said that Matthew changed the ending, right?"

Loretta rolled back toward her friends. "That's right. Sofia told him to do it."

"The hero uses her magic power to save the day," Darcy said. "She didn't know she had the power, but she finds it anyway. When she needs it most."

"Not much of a clue," Jisha said.

"Maybe it's not a clue," Darcy said. "I mean, clues are supposed to lead you to something. But this is better than a clue. It's a set of instructions. It's telling you exactly what to do."

"Do *what*?" Loretta asked.

"I don't know!"

"We might be overthinking this," Jisha said. "Maybe it's just the ending that Matthew and Sofia came up with because they thought it was cool. End of story."

A week ago, Loretta would have accepted Jisha's explanation. But so much had changed.

"Maybe it's a clue, maybe it isn't," Loretta said. "I guess I just felt safer with all of you here."

Claire began to snore.

"Even you, Claire."

Darcy laughed so loud that she snorted, which woke Claire. "What?" Claire asked.

They each told Loretta, in their own way, that Matthew and Sofia would come home, and that she did the right thing by shooting the movie for them. It would have been wrong to put it aside.

"You did a good thing," Darcy said.

Eventually, their voices died out. They were all asleep.

The bears came to life. Rana unsheathed her sword. Without a word, the juro followed Spark to the staircase.

TWENTY-FOUR

Sir Reginald must have heard them coming. He stood half-way out of the closet, his beady eyes reflecting the nightlight. Silently, the bears regrouped in Loretta's room, forming a circle at the foot of the bed. Rana joined them, though she seemed amused at their ritual, as if she were the adult and they were children playing make-believe. Zed stayed close to the door in case he needed to run away.

"I was really lookin' forward to this," Lulu said. "And then you call a juro."

"We're not happy about it, either," Spark said.

"Listen," Sir Reginald said. "This monster we're fighting: I have never seen anything like it. But I have heard of him. As a matter of fact, he used to be one of us."

He laid it out for them, from the recent attacks on Loretta to Matthew's kidnapping. Only Ozzie had heard the story of Jakmal, though they all knew of the old days, when monsters roamed freely, before the League finally reined them in.

"Jakmal must be very sad," Ozzie said.

Everyone looked at him. "I know," he said. "We're not here to make him feel better."

"You're right, though," Spark said. "He *is* sad. I wish we could help him. Maybe someday. But we have to stop him first."

Sir Reginald told them about the scratcher—what it did, how it worked. "Who knows how many of these machines are out there, punching holes in our world?" he said.

Spark asked Rana if the monster she fought used a scratcher. "I guess he did," she said. "But I never saw it."

Spark told them to wait while she fetched something from the attic. Minutes later, she returned with a bedsheet tucked beneath her arm. She placed it on the floor and unrolled it. Lying flat, the sheet revealed the armor she had constructed.

"Whoa," Lulu said.

The bears strapped on the leather vests, along with the spiked ankle and wrist guards. Ozzie stuck out his fist, pretending to jab a monster with it. Lulu checked out her new armor in the mirror, grinning. Rana popped her head through the collar of the vest and then adjusted the leather strap.

"How do we know if Jakmal will appear tonight?" Ozzie asked.

"We don't," Spark said. "But we know where he likes to scratch. And that's where we lay our trap."

She asked them to take something from their dusas— something important to them. Jakmal could sense what the children desired, and what they feared. Bringing these objects to a single place could attract the monster—or at least, that's what the bears had come to believe, based on the stories that the League passed down through the ages.

They brought the objects to Loretta's room and laid them on the carpet. Lulu took Jisha's baseball cap. Ozzie swiped Darcy's fingerless gloves, which she had knitted herself. Rana took Claire's new watch.

"We should get some of Matthew's things while we're at it," Spark said. "That's where Lulu comes in."

"Me?"

Spark reminded Lulu of the time she stole from Jisha's parents, after they wrongfully took away her allowance.

"You're not supposed to do that," Zed said, as always.

"It wasn't fair!" Lulu replied.

They needed Lulu to break into Matthew's room and retrieve a few items. Sir Reginald listed them: a lock of hair from a photo album, the pillowcases, and his favorite T-shirt.

"Don't you need special tools to pick locks?" Ozzie asked.

Lulu smiled. She stuffed her right paw inside her left armpit and pulled out a bobby pin. She reached inside again and revealed a metal sliver shaped like a toothpick.

"Oh, come on," she said. "Y'all don't have these things handy?"

"You're not supposed to do that," Spark said, chuckling.

"We'll put the items in this corner," Sir Reginald said. "That's where he likes to scratch."

Rana laughed. "Are you sure you're not imagining all this? Claire had a bear before me, and he used to talk about this stuff all the time."

"Perhaps he was trying to warn you," Sir Reginald said.

"Maybe. But as soon as that bear was gone, the monsters went away, too. What a coincidence."

"Didn't you see the car outside?" Spark said.

"Yes. A branch fell on it."

"Rana, listen. We need you. You're the only one who's killed one of these things."

"I said I'll help you. I just wonder if you and the old bear here are letting your imaginations run wild. How many of these silly movies have you made with your human?"

"When we see Jakmal tonight," Sir Reginald said, "then you can tell me if we are imagining things."

"I don't care if this beast is real or not," Ozzie said. "We live by a code. We are bound to it, even if the danger has passed."

With the dispute settled for now, they ventured into the hall, where Ozzie allowed Lulu to stand on his shoulders while she fiddled with the keyhole. The others lined the wall, keeping watch. This proved too stressful for Zed. As expected, he retreated to Loretta's room.

"Zed!" Spark whispered. "We could use another hand."

"What?"

"You could *try* to fight with us."

The monkey stopped at the door. "I'm sorry. I just can't." He ran to the closet and locked himself inside.

In the dead of night, the scraping of metal against metal sounded impossibly loud. Something moved in Mom and Dad's room. Lulu stopped and listened. After a minute, the parents settled in again, both snoring. Lulu continued.

When the door finally popped open, a musty draft filtered out. The warriors filed inside, with Sir Reginald leading the way. He pointed to the pillows. Ozzie hopped onto the bed and stripped the cases. Spark and Lulu rummaged through the

149

drawer until they found the shirt they needed. It had a movie projector logo, with the words YOUNG FILMMAKERS AWARD stenciled on the front. Despite the passage of time, it still smelled like Matthew. Sir Reginald opened the photo album on the desk. When he found the lock of hair, he ripped it from the page, pulling away a strip of Scotch tape.

It felt so wrong to be in here. Mom and Dad had locked the door so they wouldn't be reminded of Matthew every time they walked by. If they were to ever catch the bears sneaking around, Spark hoped it would not be at this moment, when she trespassed in this space they had set aside.

On the way out, Spark stopped and glanced inside the closet. She walked over to the doorframe and dropped to her knees. Sliding the toy chest aside, she found the symbol that Sir Reginald had carved into the wood—the circle with two bear paws inside. One held a sword, the other a lightning bolt, though it took some imagination to recognize it. Spark rubbed her paw over the symbol, then slid the box into place.

"Come on, Hotshot," Sir Reginald said.

"I'm right behind you," she said.

The juro returned to Loretta's room and placed the objects in a triangle. The warriors then chose their weapons. Spark loaded the nail gun. Sir Reginald brandished Arctos. Ozzie lifted the circular saw. Lulu tested the slingshot. Rana twirled her sword like a cheerleader's baton.

Spark told them to each take a dumbbell. Each weight was tied to the radiator with a rope, which would act as an anchor to keep the portal open. Holding the rift open was the key to the plan—without it, they could not lure the monster into the attic. And even worse, Jakmal would be able to disappear and reappear at will.

"Now," Sir Reginald said, "when this rift appears, we will see Jakmal's dungeon. It is a terrible place. Do not let it distract you."

They held their weapons tighter.

"There may be an opportunity to get inside," he added. "To see what he's been doing."

"Wait a minute," Spark said.

Sir Reginald kept going. "This may be our only chance. He could have more children in there. We might even see some of them. Or hear them."

"More children," Ozzie whispered.

"Sir Reginald," Spark said, "may I speak with you? Alone?"

He glared at her. "Jakmal could be here any minute."

"We'll make it quick."

Sir Reginald approached her. Behind him, the puzzled warriors glanced at each other. Spark led him to the other side of the bed.

"We talked about this," she said. "We're not going into the rift unless *I* give the order."

"I have been thinking," he said. "We could create a diversion. If we distract the monster, we can—"

"No," Spark said. "We stick to the plan we agreed on."

"We can't rule it out."

"*I'm* ruling it out."

Sir Reginald scrunched his snout.

"*I* called the juro," Spark said.

"You would not even know what a juro is if it were not for me."

"And you wouldn't be standing here if it weren't for *me*."

Sir Reginald stamped his foot.

"We can't have two people in charge," she said. "Right or wrong, I'm calling the shots."

"Calling the shots," he hissed. "You mean telling us to retreat. You think that is what the Founders would have wanted?"

"I don't care what the Founders wanted."

Sir Reginald flinched, as if Spark had slapped him in the face.

"That symbol you carved in the floor is still there," Spark said. "One paw holds a sword, the other holds a lightning bolt."

Sir Reginald waited.

"One paw belongs to a general, the other to a hexen," she said. "*They're* the Founders, aren't they? They're the ones who betrayed Jakmal."

His shoulders slumped. She couldn't have been the first bear to figure it out, and to ask him about it. It must have broken his heart every time.

"That is true," he said.

"What else did the Founders lie about?"

"Spark—"

"'Bears watch, always and forever.' Is that a lie, too?"

"Stop."

"I'm not a cub anymore, Sir. I deserve to know the truth. All of it."

On the other side of the bed, Lulu whistled aimlessly. She wanted them to hurry. But Spark would not budge.

"Go ahead and tell on me to the Grand Sleuth," Spark said.

"No one has heard from the Grand Sleuth in years," Sir Reginald said, lowering his gaze.

Spark got closer to him so he could whisper whatever he needed to say next.

"You wanted the truth," he said. "Here it is. The council is either in hiding, or it has been destroyed. I fear that something terrible has happened. A new wave of monsters. We are on our own."

"Wait. You said destroyed. What do you mean?"

"I told you once that bears were special," he said. "That we could not be discarded like the other toys. That the Grand Sleuth could grant us the power to live on."

"Yes."

"We have no reason to believe that that's true."

"What are you saying?"

"We help our dusa move forward in life. It is our purpose. But the day always comes when we are no longer needed. Ever again. And then we just . . . fade away."

"You mean . . . we die?"

"Yes. That is what 'final light' means in the oath. It is the day we are left behind."

Spark glanced at the others to make sure they could not hear. "But you weren't left behind. You've served two generations of this family."

"I was lucky. Most of us are not."

She imagined lying limp on the attic floor, gathering dust, along with all the other unwanted things.

"That's how I know Matthew is alive," Sir Reginald said. "Because I'm still here. His love brought me to life. And it keeps me alive."

"So all that stuff about the Grand Sleuth calling on me . . ."

Sir Reginald could not bring himself to say it. He merely shook his head no.

This new revelation left Spark dizzy. She tried to focus her jumbled thoughts. "Forget the Grand Sleuth," she said. "If Matthew's definitely alive, then maybe Sofia is, too."

"Spark—"

"We'll pry open this portal and storm that castle if we have to!"

"That's not what I'm asking," Sir Reginald said. "You should proceed with your plan. But if I see a chance, I will go in myself. If I fail, then you must destroy the scratcher. Cut our losses."

"Sir—"

"This is the only way. If we all go in and get lost in there, then four more children will go missing. And if we hold that portal open too long, there's no telling what it will do."

On the far side of the room, the others whispered among themselves, asking what was taking so long.

"Just one question," Spark said. "If you find Matthew, can you stop the final light?"

"I cannot stop it. Even if I save him. But if it is going to happen, I would like to see him one more time."

A wave of fear rippled through Spark. She trembled. But then she imagined Loretta, years from now. A teenager, and then a woman. Fearless. Safe. A loving person. And the despair began to drift away, until it felt as if she had known all along that this was the truth.

"I wanted to tell you sooner," Sir Reginald said. "When I thought you were ready. The League keeps it a secret so we won't stray from our mission. Only a few bears know. And some days, I wish I had never found out."

"It's okay," Spark said. "I'm glad you told me. I can't worry about what might happen. When the final light will come. Our friends need our help. If this is our purpose, then so be it."

"You're not afraid?"

"Of course I'm afraid. But like you said: it doesn't matter who made us. It doesn't matter where we're going. What matters is what we do *now*."

Sir Reginald eyed her, annoyed but also proud that she had turned his own words against him.

She stuck out her paw. The old bear squeezed it. "You have my sword," he said. "Until the final light."

They rejoined the others. Thankfully, no one asked any questions. Spark wondered how many of them knew the truth. How many of them realized that their time was so short.

She took her place at the front, as if she were the tip of a great spear. Which she was.

TWENTY-FIVE

In the deepest, darkest part of the night, long after the colors had bled away and the sounds had faded to silence, a distinct odor of rust and grease wafted through the room. One by one, the warriors perked up. They raised their weapons. Rana, the last to notice the scent, lifted her sword over her shoulder.

Something scraped against the walls. The corner of the room shimmered, like a mirage in the desert. Spark blinked a few times to make sure she was not imagining it. And then the portal opened, and orange light burst forth from the blackness, swallowing part of the floor and the walls. A hot wind blew in Spark's face. Neither Mom nor Dad, nor the children downstairs, would hear any of it, thanks to the muffle spell. The defenders of this house were on their own.

"Cables," Spark said.

Each of the warriors took a dumbbell and tossed it. Five ropes stretched out and tightened against the edges of the bubble. As the portal expanded, Spark caught a glimpse of the first floor of the house, where Loretta slept on the floor with her friends. Above, at the unstable boundaries of the rift, she saw the attic ceiling.

"Let's say the words," she said. "We are . . . Spark . . ."

They took turns speaking their names.

"Sir Reginald."

"Lulu."

"Ozzie."

"Rana, Amazon Princess."

They spoke in unison: "We are the sworn protectors of this house. We serve goodness and truth. We give refuge to the innocent. We defend the light . . . to the *final* light . . . in times of darkness. By the power bestowed upon us by the League of Ursus, we command you to be gone."

The final light, Spark thought. Perhaps hers had come. Until then, she was here, holding her weapon, ready to fight.

Clanking noises—like machines in a factory—echoed from the gateway. Spark drew closer until she saw the castle at the base of a volcanic mountain, with a moat made of lava. Torches burned on walls made of stone. Her stomach fluttered when she realized that the portal hovered slightly above the highest tower. She stretched her neck to see all the way down the slope, at least sixty feet, to the base of the castle. From what she could tell, the device opened the portal onto the mountain, making the attic feel like a cave in the steep rock face.

"Do you see the scratcher?" Sir Reginald asked.

Spark crawled on all fours toward the opening. At the very edge, where she could feel the steam from the lava brush against her face, she heard a familiar hissing sound.

"He's here."

An enormous form rose above the edge of the rift. Like before, Jakmal placed his feet onto the hardwood floor, one at a time. Only now, the clawlike feet had grown to the size of giant crabs. Behind her, the others gasped at the sight. Jakmal stared at the small army that greeted him, squinting his enormous black eyes. He rose to such a height that his horns brushed against the ceiling. The pendant with the face on it rested against his chest, the eyelids sealed, the jaw hanging open. Jakmal grinned, revealing his fangs. A line of spit drooled from his lips.

Someone let out a bloodcurdling scream, so loud that even Jakmal flinched. Spark glanced behind her to see Rana, her mouth agape. The Amazon Princess ran to the closet door and pounded on it. "Let me in! You stupid monkey, let me in!"

The closet door opened a mere crack. Rana squeezed inside and pulled it shut.

Spark watched all of this with eyes so wide they almost dropped out of her head.

"I don't think she's killed a monster before," Ozzie said.

Jakmal growled at them. A rock caromed off his forehead. He raised his hand for cover while Lulu reloaded her slingshot. Spark aimed the gun and fired. A nail whistled through the air and landed in Jakmal's shoulder. While he tried to yank it out, Sir Reginald charged, driving his sword into one of Jakmal's legs. Unfazed, the monster lifted the tiny bear and tossed him across the room. Sir Reginald landed on the nightstand, knocking the lamp onto the mattress.

Jakmal swung his tail at Ozzie. The polar bear pressed the trigger on the saw in the nick of time. The blade squealed, shooting out tiny red embers. The force of it knocked Ozzie over, sending him skidding across the hardwood.

Even with Spark firing the nail gun, Jakmal kept getting closer, until one of his feet tripped on a rope. After a quick glance at the cables, the monster crawled into the rift and vanished. Everything became quiet again.

With a strange howling sound, the portal moved. It slinked along the floor and up the wall, tugging the ropes with it.

Sir Reginald got to his feet and retrieved his sword. "He's trying to cut the lines!"

Right on cue, one of the ropes snapped.

"We have to keep the portal open!" Spark said.

"Grab a rope," Sir Reginald said. "Don't let go!"

The portal moved from the wall to the ceiling, lifting the ropes. Holding on with one paw, Spark felt herself rise from the floor. Above her, the edges of the rift wobbled, like heat rising from hot asphalt. The bears dangled over the bed. Sir Reginald held his sword in his teeth as he shimmied his way up. Spark bumped against Ozzie's feet, while her own feet brushed the crown of Lulu's head.

With a sudden jerking movement, the portal drew them in. The orange glow faded, leaving only blackness. Spark closed her eyes, felt herself spinning, somersaulting. A burning wind screamed in her ears.

TWENTY-SIX

When Spark opened her eyes again, she found herself on the floor of the attic, still gripping the nail gun. The plan had worked so far. The portal pulled them into Jakmal's world for a moment, long enough for them to pass through the ceiling, just like it did with Sir Reginald.

A few feet away, Ozzie helped Lulu stand. Sir Reginald walked past Spark, following the single remaining rope as it snaked toward the other end of the room. The others trailed behind him, each grabbing a section before it could get away. The line jerked to the left, sliding a cardboard box with it.

"Hold on," Sir Reginald said.

Behind the barricades, Spark could see the orange glow once more. There, in the corner, the rope started to disappear into the portal, which was now a tiny hole in the floor, barely large enough for a mouse. The portal zigzagged, as if it were trying to shake off the rope.

"Pull," Spark said.

The line emerged from the opening a few inches at a time.

Something tugged the other end of the rope, hard. The bears fell forward, their bellies dragging along the wood. Sir Reginald and Spark arrived at the portal first, while the rope burned through their paws. With Lulu and Ozzie struggling behind her, Spark aimed the nail gun into the opening and fired again and again, grunting each time.

"Come on!" she screamed. "Come fight us, you coward!"

The portal burst open, sending all four of them flying in different directions. Jakmal crawled out, his white skin bathed in the orange glow. Behind him, the wall and ceiling vanished. The chasm opened even wider, revealing the fortress and the burning wasteland beyond.

The monster clenched his fists. His head swiveled toward something on the floor. It was Lulu, taking shelter behind one of the barricades. Jakmal grabbed her, knocking her slingshot away. He bared his teeth when Lulu's spiked armor cut into his hand. With his sharp fingernails, Jakmal prepared to rip into her soft belly.

Meanwhile, on the other side of the room, a lit fuse crackled. Ozzie hid behind the row of plastic tubes, lighter in hand, a big smile on his face.

And Jakmal would soon regret casting his muffle spell.

It was too late to get out of the way. A rocket streaked across the room and exploded against his shoulder, thudding like a machine gun. *Buh-buh-buh-buh-buh-boom-boom-boom-boom!* The flashes blinded Spark for a few seconds. Next to her, Lulu fell to the ground and patted out a small fire on her coat.

When the explosions stopped, Jakmal clutched a burn mark on his collarbone. Part of his chain mail had been blasted away, the broken links still red-hot.

Spark lifted the nail gun. "Charge!"

Ozzie carried one of the firecracker pipes on his shoulder, like a bazooka, with the fuse crackling again. Lulu somersaulted to dodge a slash from Jakmal's tail. She landed near the slingshot, scooped it up, and fired a sharp rock that grazed the monster's cheek. Sir Reginald leapt onto Jakmal's wounded shoulder and drove his sword into the exposed skin. The monster screeched. As the bear tried to dig the blade out for another strike, Jakmal's pincered tail snatched him and tossed him away.

The second rocket fired. This one flew over Jakmal's head and disappeared into the void. Moving faster now, the monster swiped the tube from Ozzie. The bear tried to retreat, but Jakmal swung the tube and batted him across the room. He tumbled into the stairwell.

Another rock bounced off Jakmal's jaw. Hiding in one of the trenches, Lulu reloaded her slingshot. When Jakmal spotted her, he gripped the dresser in the corner of the room, lifted it, and slammed it on top of the trench, trapping her inside. Spark aimed and fired. Two more nails pierced the base of the monster's neck. But then the gun went *click*. Empty.

"There it is!" Sir Reginald shouted. "It's on the turret! Look!"

A beam of light shot out from the side of the castle. The source of the light appeared harmless enough. It was a black metal box about the size of a filing cabinet, with a steel tube sticking out of the front. At the end of the tube, a crystal glowed bright white, as if a star was trapped inside, threatening to burst out. The machine hummed like a human voice. Spark almost laughed when she realized that the scratcher resembled a projector, and the portal it created appeared like a movie screen, the image imprinted on the side of the mountain.

Jakmal must have realized then what they were trying to do. Using the pincer on the end of his tail, he snagged the last remaining cable and cut it with one snap. The rope slid away into the rift.

There would be no rescue mission now. The best they could hope for was to stop this monster, if that was even possible.

Spark raced to the firecrackers. If she could aim one at the scratcher, she could shut it down for good. As she ran, something large and heavy whizzed over her head and crashed against the wall. She turned to see Jakmal lifting a second box full of junk, the family's memories. He hurled it at her. She rolled out of the way as it slid past.

Spark took cover behind a stack of boxes. A few feet away, Lulu emerged from a hole in the floor, having crawled through the rafters. Ozzie retreated behind the thick leg of a desk, where his circular saw waited for him.

"Slow him down for me," Spark said. "I'm going for the rocket."

The bears nodded. Spark took off in a full sprint. Ozzie and Lulu charged the monster, screaming. She loved them for it.

Spark climbed onto the workbench. A Zippo lighter rested against one of the tubes. As she tried to strike the flame, she glanced at the battle taking place before her. Lulu clung to the monster, punching him with her little paws. The whining of Ozzie's electric saw changed pitch as it cut into Jakmal's scales. Sir Reginald leapt onto the back of his neck, brandishing Arctos. And then, arriving from nowhere, a fourth creature landed on Jakmal's armor.

The long tail gave it away.

"Monkey?" Spark shouted.

Zed held a weapon his hands. Rana's little metal sword! He wielded it like a warrior, hacking at Jakmal's arms. The monster writhed and twisted. The claw on his tail snapped like a viper. As they fought, the portal widened to engulf nearly half the attic. Soon it would swallow all of them, maybe drag the entire house with it.

Sir Reginald dove away from Jakmal. The tail lashed at him and missed. At the edge of the portal, the bear jammed his paw into the stitches on his side and pulled the yarn from the wound.

Jakmal finally got his hands on Ozzie. Before he could rip the little bear apart, Lulu jumped onto the crown of Jakmal's skull and pummeled his face with her stubby fists. She distracted him long enough for Zed to drive his sword into a gap in the monster's chain mail.

Spark watched as Sir Reginald tied the yarn from his wound to a loose nail on a floorboard. This was the chance he was waiting for. She knew he would never wait for an order, because in his position, neither would she. With the line secure, the bear did a swan dive into the portal, the string trailing behind him.

Sensing danger, Jakmal dropped Ozzie and shrugged off Lulu. He snapped his tail, which threw Zed upward, bouncing him off the ceiling. Jakmal spun around to face the rift. Spark could no longer see Sir Reginald, only the thin line that connected him to this world.

With a tube tucked under each arm and the lighter in her mouth, Spark jumped down from the workbench and rejoined the others. Ozzie held in the stuffing that had come loose from his torso. Lulu patted herself to make sure everything was okay. Though lying flat on his stomach, Zed lifted his head, dazed yet still alive. They were so brave, Spark thought. They answered the call, like the noble warriors they were.

From the edge of the portal, Spark could see it all clearly now. Sir Reginald's yarn extended from the floorboard all the way down the mountain to the castle's drawbridge. It must have been a forty-foot drop before he hit the first rock and then bounced the rest of the way. Above him, in the highest turret, the scratcher continued its eerie projection. Jakmal bounded down the steep mountainside toward the castle moat.

Spark dropped one of the tubes on the floor and spit the lighter into her palm.

"What are you doing?" Lulu said.

"I'm going after them."

She flicked the lighter open and struck it to make sure it worked. Then she clicked it shut.

"Do not follow me. Do you understand? No matter what happens, don't come after me. If he takes me, then use the rocket to destroy the scratcher. Got it?"

Lulu and Zed nodded. It took a few more seconds for Ozzie to do the same.

Spark stared into the void. She was not ready to jump. She jumped anyway.

She fell and fell and fell, down the mountainside. The tower rose beside her, its lava moat bubbling and frothing. Spark landed on a rock, tumbled. The tube and the lighter slipped from her grasp. She regained her footing on a ledge right above Jakmal. The monster spotted her, his pale face twisting in rage. As he reached for her, an enormous object fell from above and crashed on top of him. It took a moment for Spark to realize that her friends had dropped a cardboard box full of old china. The shattered contents spilled out, bits of shiny porcelain bouncing from the rocks. The box lay crumpled on Jakmal's limp body.

The monster grumbled.

Spark jumped from the ledge and followed the yarn into the tower. The thread pulled tight around the chains that held the drawbridge. She ran across, through a wave of heat rising from the lava and into the dark mouth of the castle.

TWENTY-SEVEN

The castle gate led into a hallway with a vaulted ceiling and mounted torches lighting the path. The flames left black scorch marks on the stones above. The cobblestones felt warm underfoot.

In the flickering light, Spark followed the thread past a row of enormous doors. When she shouted Sir Reginald's name, her voice echoed through the hallway. The corridor stretched on and on before her, vanishing in a small dot far, far away. An infinite span of cobblestones, with an infinite number of chambers. It was impossible—the castle was not big enough for it. And yet she remembered what Sir Reginald told her: *The tower is some kind of gateway.* A gateway from nowhere to everywhere.

The yarn lifted from the ground, stretching tight against one of the archways. Spark followed it to find another door, hanging open a few inches, with the yarn sneaking through.

As soon as she pushed the door in, her foot landed on a soft carpet. She entered a room much like the den at home, with a bookshelf and an enormous, soft recliner. The chair faced away from her, toward a flickering television. On the screen, men shouted and water splashed about while ominous music played in the background. She recognized the movie right away. It was *Jaws*. She arrived at the moment when Chief Brody and his friends try to shoot harpoons into the giant shark. Everything about this room made her think of home. It was the warmth. And a scent she recognized. Blueberries. Blueberry waffles! She spotted a plate of crumbs on a table beside the chair. This safe feeling wrapped around her, the way it did when the family would gather on a Friday night and doze off while watching some zombie movie.

The recliner tilted a bit. Someone was sitting in it. Spark retreated to the doorframe. A figure shuffled out of the chair, appearing only as a shadow against the flashing screen. It was a boy. *Matthew!*

He noticed something on the floor. A piece of cloth with a long string attached to it. With his strong hand, Matthew lifted it, held it in the light. His old teddy bear, Sir Reginald the Brave, stared back at him. In the boy's sunken eyes, Spark recognized a sort of giddy disbelief. How could this be, he must have thought. Matthew's oldest friend had come to find him.

Sir Reginald did not move. Without his stuffing, his body had deflated into a furry rag.

Spark felt the ground shake. A strange clicking sound echoed through the castle, moving closer. She peeked into the hall. Jakmal waited at the main gate, standing so tall that his head nearly touched the archway. He pulled a lever attached to the wall. Beside it, a heavy chain moved from the ceiling to the floor, each link clanging against the cobblestones.

The drawbridge slowly lifted. In a few moments, it would seal them all inside.

Without thinking, without a plan, Spark leapt onto one of the torches and yanked it loose. It clattered to the floor. She grabbed it and ran full speed at Jakmal. The beast heard something coming and spun around so quickly that his tail slapped against the wall.

Aiming right at the creepy necklace on his chest, Spark flung the torch. The flame struck Jakmal's hide and burst into a bright cloud of embers. A terrible shriek cut through the air, a sound the creature had never made before. Jakmal covered the strange face on his chest with his hands, like a mother cradling a baby. Slowly, the two eyes on the face opened. They glared at Spark, cursing her for what she did. The mouth tightened with rage, ready to scream again.

Spark understood now. The knight's brother did not die from wounds. No, the hexen's spell did something far worse. It fused the two brothers into one hideous body. The knight named Jak, and his brother . . . Mal. An abomination, twisted in agony and bent on revenge.

And it was coming right for her.

Spark fled into the hallway, past Matthew's room, where the door remained slightly open. Jakmal gave chase, snorting and howling, his claws scraping against the ground. He sounded like an avalanche rolling toward her.

Spark glanced behind her, past the monster rumbling through the hall. She saw Matthew sneaking out, still clutching Sir Reginald. In a daze, he headed for the drawbridge, which had risen halfway to the top. He could make it. Spark wouldn't.

So be it. She ran faster now, into the endless corridor. *Come find me now*, she thought. *Come get lost in here with me.*

And before long, she noticed that she could hear only her own footsteps, nothing else.

She stopped and turned around. Jakmal now ran in the opposite direction, his tail waving with each lumbering step he took. He was going after Matthew.

Spark followed. The torches zipped by as she tried to catch up, but the hallway seemed to get longer and longer. The chains on the bridge continued to clink, the sound growing louder. Jakmal reached the drawbridge as it tilted diagonally. Not even bothering to stop the bridge from lifting, he slithered through the opening and launched himself from the edge. The wood shivered under his weight.

The drawbridge stood nearly vertical by the time Spark hopped onto one of its crossbeams and pulled herself to the top. She tried to stick her paw through the opening, but the bridge slammed shut, letting in a puff of hot air. Spark slid from the top and bounced onto the floor. She pounded her paws on the wood. It would not give an inch.

She stopped and listened. She could hear only the crackling torches. Everything else remained still. A coldness settled into her belly, freezing her legs in place. She was trapped.

TWENTY-EIGHT

After a minute of pulling and heaving, Spark finally accepted that the lever controlling the drawbridge would never budge. She tried hanging from it, she tried wedging her body against it. Nothing worked. Jakmal had built the handle so that only a giant's hand could move it.

Suddenly, her strength began to leave her, like air escaping a balloon. She dropped to the floor. Her limbs stiffened, her paws hardened into little bricks. There was something about this place that sapped her energy. *No*, she thought. *It's not time yet. It's not final light. I still need to—*

To what? She tried to focus. Loretta. She needed to save Loretta. In her hazy memory, she tried to recall the things Sir Reginald trained her to do. "You always have choices," he would say. "Find out what they are. Know your surroundings. Know what you can do." For a moment, she imagined herself gathering the torches, maybe lifting one of the cobblestones loose—anything she could use as a weapon. She would wait for Jakmal when the drawbridge opened again. No element of surprise, no traps, just a straight fight.

But no. No, she could hardly match him with three other bears and a monkey. She gazed into the endless corridor. Sir Reginald's advice did not apply here. When the monster returned, he would have no use for her. She would go on a mantelpiece somewhere. Or in a pile of firewood.

But it would never come to that, would it? Once Jakmal found Loretta, Spark would not last much longer. *Their love gives us strength*, Sir Reginald once told her. *And in return, we protect them.* It all seemed like a joke now. The bears could not really protect anyone. There were too many monsters out there, prowling, seeking out weak spots. The bears could only hold the line and wait. They could only make their dusas *feel* safe, nothing more. How did it get like this, she wondered. How did the monsters enjoy so many advantages, while the heroes could use only firecrackers and slingshots to fight them? How did the monsters get claws and scratchers, and a castle with doorways to everywhere—

Doorways, she thought. Doorways. Yes. Jakmal scratched all around the house, hadn't he? In the attic, in the bedrooms.

One of these doorways could take her home.

With great effort, she rolled onto her side and crawled deeper into the corridor. She came to the first door and pulled herself to her feet. The knob seemed so far away. She tried jumping, but couldn't make it. It was like she was soaked in water again. Exhausted, she gripped the doorframe and climbed. When she got close enough to reach the knob, she grabbed hold and let the weight of her body turn it. The door squeaked open. Inside was an empty chamber—a tiny room that did not yet have a portal.

It went on like this for the other chambers until she opened a door that led to a closet in someone's house. She could tell right away that it led back to her world—though somewhere far away from home, maybe in another country. This was what the castle could do, just like Sir Reginald had said. The tower's walls could seal in the portals that the scratcher created, so that the monster could haunt all of the dark and unknown places that terrified children.

Shuddering, Spark closed the door and moved on to the next one. It led to a garage. The one after that opened at the base of a dead tree in the middle of a forest. She heard an owl hooting, and crickets chirping. Then she opened a door that led to a bedroom where sunlight streamed in through the window. A voice spoke on a radio in a language she did not understand. A room on the other side of the world, where morning broke.

There was no time to check all the rooms. Impossible, she thought. Impossible. She knelt on the floor, her paws on her knees.

With the last of her strength, she screamed Loretta's name so loud that the sound ricocheted through the corridor.

It was against the rules to speak to a dusa. But the Grand Sleuth wasn't here to scold her.

The echo died out. An eerie silence drifted over her. She lowered her head.

"Hello?" a faint voice called out from deep in the tunnel. The voice was groggy, confused. The voice of a girl unsure if she was still dreaming.

"Loretta," Spark whispered.

"Who's there?"

Other voices joined in.

"What's wrong, Lor?"

"Did you hear that?" Loretta said.

"Hear what?"

The girls remained still. Loretta held her breath. And then Jisha clamped her palms to her mouth and made a fart noise, as loud as a trumpet, and they all burst into uncontrollable laughter.

Spark became giddy. No matter how far apart they were, they could still hear each other, even in a place like this. And this time, Loretta would save *her*.

Spark stood awkwardly. Though still dazed, she could make it. Leaning on the wall, she trudged further into the corridor, toward the sound of her dusa's voice.

"Where are you going?" Darcy asked. The voice was closer this time.

Spark could hear them walking through the house. After years of living there, she could pinpoint their location by the pitch of the creaking floorboards. Loretta took the lead, running her hands along the wall, blindly feeling for a doorway that couldn't possibly be there. She moved from the living room to the kitchen to the top of the basement stairs.

"Keep going!" Spark shouted.

The girls descended the staircase. At the same time, Spark arrived at a door and planted her ear against it. She could hear the stairs squeaking. This was the one. The way home. She opened it, ran inside—

—and crashed into a brick wall. This room was a mere closet.

"Oh no," Spark said.

Loretta heard her. "What do I do?"

"Who are you talking to?" Jisha asked.

"What is going *on*?" That had to be Claire.

Spark understood now. Jakmal planned to use this room to get to the lower level of the house. He had linked this doorway to the basement, maybe when he was probing for ways to get in. But he had not completed a stable portal for it. Only the scratcher could do that.

The scratcher, she thought. She remembered what Sir Reginald had said: *It takes a special kind of power to use the scratcher.*

It was amazing how a crazy idea could make perfect sense when there was nothing else left.

"Loretta, concentrate on my voice. Can you hear it?"

Loretta did not answer. She didn't have to. Spark could feel her dusa's presence.

"You can reach me if you try," Spark said. "It's like . . ."

It was like the movie. She needed to use her power, just like the hero did.

"Loretta," Darcy said, her voice trembling. "Loretta, you're scaring me."

A tremor shook the castle. Spark almost lost her balance. Another quake knocked a torch to the ground. Mortar crumbled from the ceiling. And then a high-pitched squeal, like a siren, howled through the corridor. Spark clamped her paws to her ears to block the noise.

The room expanded, like a balloon taking in air. Brick by brick, the far wall fell away. As the siren died out, a hole opened, barely large enough for Spark to fit through. The doorway now led straight into the basement. She gaped at the sight. It was impossible, but it was no miracle. Loretta had done it, and didn't even seem to realize it. She was the one this monster wanted. She was the special one.

Darcy switched on the lamp. Her friends shielded their eyes from the brightness. All except Loretta, who held out her hands and spread her fingers, forcing the portal open. She grimaced. Her arm muscles strained.

None of them noticed the portal, which appeared in the corner of the room, between Dad's workbench and a chair.

Darcy tapped Loretta's arm. "Are you all right?"

Jisha got closer, though not too close. "I think she's sleep-walking."

Loretta balled her hands into fists and dropped to her knees. Darcy caught her before she completely toppled over. "Oh my God, *Lor!*"

Her friends gathered around her. Loretta took a deep, loud breath, like a diver coming up for air.

"Matthew," she gasped. "Matthew's here."

"She's hallucinating," Claire said.

"We have to find him," Loretta said.

Spark wanted nothing more than to join them. Maybe this would be her last chance. But she had work to do. Her strength had returned. Her body felt like a coiled spring. Final light would have to wait. She charged through the tiny portal, right past Loretta's feet. Before anyone could catch a glimpse of her, Spark yanked the lamp's cord from its socket. The room went completely dark.

Claire screamed. "What was that?"

"What was what?" Darcy said.

"It went up the stairs!"

Spark kept running. She knew the way, even in the blackness. The girls' voices faded as she made her way to the attic door. She hopped onto the knob and turned it, feeling the latch click. The orange glow filled the stairwell as the door opened. Only a few feet from the entrance, the attic floor dropped away into Jakmal's world, as if a giant movie screen hung from the ceiling. Her friends—the two bears and the monkey—stood as black shadows along the edge, gazing at the castle.

Sir Reginald's thread still hung from the nail in the floorboard. Ozzie gripped the line and prepared to climb down the mountain. The others helped him as he placed his first foot over the edge.

"I thought I said *don't* go into the rift!" Spark said.

They all froze. Zed and Lulu stepped away from her, as if she were a ghost. Ozzie slipped a bit before regaining his footing. "Wait," he said, "how did you . . . ?"

"I'll explain later. Where's Matthew?"

Lulu pointed. Below, Matthew hid in a jagged crater, having made it halfway up the slope of the mountain, almost level with the turret. He still clutched what was left of Sir Reginald. Only a few feet away, Jakmal searched for him, growling and huffing, his body wriggling like an insect. He would catch the boy in a matter of seconds.

Just outside the crater, the firecracker tube lay cracked against a boulder. Beside it, the shiny lighter reflected the glow of the lava.

"Whaddaya gonna do?" Lulu asked.

"I'm gonna make Jakmal an offer. Get ready to pull us up."

"You have to hurry," Ozzie said. "The rift is unstable. It closed all of a sudden, like that!" He tried to snap fingers that he didn't have. "And then it *opened* again a few seconds later!"

"I know," Spark said. "That's because Loretta used the scratcher."

"Loretta?"

"I'll explain that later, too."

She peered into the portal, down the mountain. The steep drop did not frighten her. That's what this Jakmal did not understand. He may have scared her at first. But that only made her stronger. And now that Loretta helped pull her into this world again, nothing could stop her.

And so she jumped.

She bounced off the boulder and rolled behind it. On the other side, Jakmal shuffled past. Crawling on all fours, Spark grabbed the lighter. She broke the firecracker tube open and shook it until the rocket slid out.

Holding the rocket in her mouth, Spark climbed the boulder. Jakmal faced away from her. His pincer wrapped around Matthew. The boy grimaced, trying to hold on to the line.

Spark lit the fuse. Jakmal heard the crackling. His head darted left and right as he searched for the noise.

Spark jumped from the rock and landed on his left shoulder, the injured one. The monster hissed. On his chest, Mal's face remained frozen. Spark grasped the rocket and jammed it into Mal's open mouth. Jak turned to her, his eyes wide with terror.

"Let him go," she said.

Mal's face remained still. Only a few inches of the wick remained.

"Time's up!" she said. "It's final light. For both of us."

Mal's eyes opened, like two long-dormant flowers finally blooming. They rolled in their sockets toward Jak, silently begging him to listen to reason.

The monster released Matthew. The boy fell to the ground in a heap. Desperate to keep moving, Matthew gripped the string again.

The wick burned to its last few centimeters. Spark would not budge. She wanted the monster to feel fear, to get a real taste of it.

At the last possible moment, she threw the rocket at the turret. Jakmal screamed as he watched the flame arcing through the air. The rocket landed beside the scratcher and exploded, shooting fire and embers from the turret. The force of it jolted the scratcher, knocking it over and shattering its glass eye. A great rumbling began, like boulders tumbling into a canyon.

The portal began to close.

Spark leapt from Jakmal and snatched the yarn, right above Matthew. "Pull!" she shouted. "Pull us up! It's closing!"

Jakmal wailed. He climbed to the turret and gazed at his broken toy. His hand hovered over the fragments of glass and metal.

Matthew and Spark continued along the rocky slope, climbing as fast as they could. The yarn guided them through clouds of smoke, where they could not see.

Something jerked the line. Spark turned to the portal and saw that it was sliding along the rock face. Inside, the bears and the monkey resembled images on a broken television screen.

"Come on!" she said.

The portal shifted to the edge of the attic. Spark could see the corner of the ceiling. In a few moments, the bubble would appear over the front of the house. "Follow me!" she screamed. Behind her, Matthew barely clung to the line. The boy was exhausted, delirious, stinking of sweat and grime.

The yarn shook violently as the portal shrank. Spark reached her arm through it as it dwindled to the size of a door. She placed her paw onto the floorboard. There, she found the bears and the monkey pulling the line with all their might. Behind them, also helping, was Rana. She glanced at Spark, her eyes begging for forgiveness.

They were now at the very edge of the attic. The bubble passed through the wall, so that part of it hung in midair over the front lawn. In its dying moments, the portal sucked in the air around them, creating a wind tunnel that toppled the boxes and coat racks. One of the overhead light bulbs burst. Still, the little heroes hung on. With their remaining strength, they gave one last tug on the line. And with that, the gateway closed, crashing shut with a great blast that knocked everyone to the floor.

Spark looked around. The others scrambled to their feet. Ozzie was the first to the window. The portal was gone. The yarn lay in a heap beside the wall. Sir Reginald may have been buried underneath.

There was no sign of Matthew.

"No," Spark said.

"Look!" Ozzie shouted.

They huddled around the window, facing the front yard. In the distance, the sun rose over the houses, burning away a thin mist. The leaves of the tree rustled. Spark thought it was the wind at first, until she saw Matthew's skinny body draped over the branches. The rapidly closing portal must have thrown him clear of the building, leaving him suspended nearly three stories in the air. His leg dangled from the limbs. The boy wiped the tears away and gazed at his home for the first time in what must have felt like ages. He was so dazed that he hardly seemed to notice when one of the branches cracked.

"He's gonna fall," Lulu said.

"Quick, open the window," Spark said. "Maybe we can reach him."

They lined up along the windowsill and tried to lift it.

"It's locked!" Ozzie said.

"I got it," Zed said. He climbed onto the polar bear's shoulders and tried to pull the lever.

"Hurry!" Spark shouted.

"It's rusted shut!"

The front door of the house burst open, and the four girls filed out, still wearing their pajamas. "Matthew!" Loretta screamed.

Another branch snapped and fell to the lawn.

Jisha pointed into the tree. "What the . . ."

Now fully alert, but not entirely sure where he was or how he got there, Matthew rolled to his side, which broke off another twig.

Loretta raced to the trunk. She grabbed the first branch and tried to pull herself up. Before she could reach the next one, Claire—the first-place rock climber!—scaled the other side so quickly that all the bears at once said, "Whoa," like they were watching a fireworks display.

Zed was so excited he slapped the window. "She climbs like a monkey!"

Claire got to Matthew first. She grabbed his shirt to keep him from tumbling to the ground. Loretta arrived second. Together, they eased Matthew down to a sturdier branch. Darcy and Jisha waited at the bottom, raising their hands as Matthew hovered over them.

Meanwhile, Zed finally jimmied the lock free.

"No," Spark said, holding the window shut. "They've got this."

Darcy and Jisha lowered Matthew to the ground. Loretta jumped from her branch and landed next to him. Matthew sat upright and reached out his arms, and they hugged each other. The other girls joined in, and they became one unit, their own juro, protecting one another.

TWENTY-NINE

With the children safe, Spark turned to the pile of yarn. She sifted through it until she found him, Sir Reginald, now a mere shell, flattened without his stuffing. His head tilted to one side, like the face on Jakmal's chest.

"Help me," Spark said.

The juro gathered the yarn in clumps and handed it over. As they collected the stuffing, something hard scraped along the floor. It was the sword Arctos, which Sir Reginald had somehow held onto until the end. Spark shoved the yarn inside of Sir Reginald, two fistfuls at a time. His belly grew fat again. His arms and legs became plump. After she stuffed the last few inches of yarn inside, she patted the wound, tried to squeeze it shut. She knelt beside him, waiting for him to move. Zed let out a little whimper, like a baby sighing. The others fell silent.

Spark nudged the old bear. "Sir Reginald." Nothing. He had fulfilled his mission.

"It's the final light," Ozzie said. He knew. Perhaps they all knew. Or had long suspected it. Either way, they could no longer deny it.

Lulu handed Spark the sword, the one she had dreamed of earning someday. On her knees, she planted the tip in the floor and leaned on the handle.

The bears, the monkey, and the princess tightened the circle around Spark. And then, one by one, they each placed a hand on her shoulder. They stayed like that for long time.

THIRTY

The front door of the house opened, and the children spilled inside. From where she sat, Spark could imagine it all: the girls surrounding Matthew, hugging him, laughing and weeping at the same time. Mom and Dad stirred from their beds and joined them. When Mom saw the boy, her lost son, she let out a whelping sound, a cry so loud and shrill that it cut Spark deep inside. Spark did not need to watch any of it for herself. She knew. She felt it. These were her people, and she was their guardian.

The juro listened as the family led Matthew into the kitchen. They fixed him a quick breakfast and peppered him with questions. He tried to answer with a mouthful of blueberry waffles. Spark could smell them.

Mom must have called the police, because soon two patrol cars arrived. The bears watched from the window as the groggy detective—the one with the thin mustache—trudged to the house holding a thermos of coffee. More people arrived, including a woman from social services and, for some reason, the fire chief. A steady stream of neighbors wandered over to the house, some so eager to see Matthew that they still wore their pajamas.

Finally, a convoy of vans blocked off the street, each with a gigantic satellite dish on its roof. A blue van with a number 10 painted on the side arrived first, followed by a white van with a number 6 and a cherry-red van with a number 3. Their side doors slid open, and out hopped the news reporters: a woman in a miniskirt, a man with impossibly white teeth, and another man with gelled hair that splashed over the top of his head like a wave. Camera operators filmed them as they spoke into their microphones. The neighbors goofed around by jumping into the shot and waving. None of the reporters seemed to mind.

More police arrived to close off the driveway with yellow tape. Three young officers guarded the lawn, each holding out their palms and telling the crowd of onlookers to stay back. Soon the police barricaded the street by parking their cars at the corner.

The detective and the social worker spoke with Matthew alone in the den. The juro tried to listen, but could barely make out the words. Meanwhile, Mom and Dad paced in the living room. It would be their turn to speak with the detective soon enough.

"Why is this taking so long?" Mom asked.

"They have to find out what's going on," Dad said. "In Matthew's own words."

She sighed. "They won't tell us anything about Sofia. They think Matthew knows something."

"He might," Dad said. "Look, it's either this, or we let them take him to the station."

"No. No, no, no. He stays here."

Mom paced some more.

"That stuff he was saying. About some monster . . ."

"He's in shock," Dad said. "He ended up climbing the tree for crying out loud."

"But he's too old to believe in all of that."

"Sometimes, when people are scared, their minds play tricks on them."

"He's old enough to know that, too."

"Julie."

"He's been through enough as it is! What if—"

"Julie!"

Mom stopped talking.

"He's alive," Dad said. "Our boy's safe. That's all that matters. We'll figure out the rest later."

Later that morning, the parents of Darcy, Jisha, and Claire pushed their way through the police blockade. The house became stuffed with people, some talking, most shouting, much like Mom and Dad's annual New Year's Eve party, but with more crying. Spark never grew tired of hearing the story, again and again, of Matthew magically appearing in the front yard. It was a story the family would repeat for the rest of their lives. It would bring them closer. It would help them see the world through each other's eyes. They would retell it in both good times and bad.

In all the commotion, no one noticed that the little movie stars had gone missing.

The noise grew louder when a new group of officers entered the house, whispering things, mumbling. They huddled in a corner with the detective while he frantically called people on his cell phone. After a few tense moments, the detective pocketed the phone and gathered the other officers.

"Okay, what is going on?" Mom shouted.

"Julie!" Dad said.

"No, I wanna know what's happening!"

"We may have found the house where your son was held captive," the detective said.

"Where?"

"It's best you stay here—"

"Don't tell me what's best for me!"

The social worker tried to calm her down. Dad told Mom that the police needed to do their jobs.

"I will get in my car and follow you if I have to," Mom said. "What're you gonna do? Arrest me?"

The detective sighed. "Fine, then follow us. It's less than a mile from here. Bring everyone if you want."

Within minutes, the house emptied. Even Claire, Jisha, and Darcy tagged along, leaving their things behind.

THIRTY-ONE

For the next hour, while the juro tried to clean the attic as best they could, sirens blared outside. Horns honked, bells rang. Police cars, ambulances, and fire trucks raced through the streets. The quiet neighborhood sounded like a city during rush hour. The juro speculated about what was going on.

"Let's check the news," Lulu said.

Spark suggested they watch on the television in Mom and Dad's room. But before they left the attic, she glanced at Sir Reginald, lying on the floor, his paws facing the ceiling.

"What about the old bear?" Lulu asked.

"He'll stay here," Spark said, tucking Arctos under her arm. "Let's go."

In the parents' room, Lulu swiped the remote from the dresser. "I watch the cooking shows when the family's not around," she said, flipping through the channels. "Can't really eat anything. But I can smell!"

She stopped on an image of the woman reporter, holding a microphone. "A dramatic turn of events today . . ."

"This is it!" Spark said. They each claimed a spot on the edge of the bed, like the front row at a movie theater.

Behind the reporter, a crowd gathered at a dilapidated house with dusty windows, a collapsed roof, and an overgrown yard. Yellow tape sealed off the front porch. Police officers stepped under it to get in and out of the door, which appeared to have been smashed in.

"Police tell us they have found a child held prisoner in this house behind me," the reporter said. "The child's name is Sofia Lopez, age thirteen—"

"Whoa," Lulu said.

Sofia's photo from the missing flyer appeared in a little box.

"Lopez was reported missing seven days ago. Police inform us that a second child, a boy, managed to escape from the house in the early morning hours. He appeared on the front doorstep of his parents' home, which is only a few blocks from here."

"That's Matthew!" Spark said.

The scene switched to a poorly lit basement with white drywall and a door that hung by its hinges, probably forced open. The camera panned to the left to find a television set, an old DVD player, and a recliner. It was the same room from the castle. Spark recalled what Sir Reginald had said about Jakmal. *My guess is that he has punched holes all over this town.* How many more were out there? How many doorways to Jakmal's world could be found in this one?

"The boy, we're told, had been missing for several days," the reporter continued. "He was obviously quite shaken. But he was able to describe for the police what he could see from the window of this room."

The reporter explained that Matthew could see the street sign for Radnor Road, along with a rusting wrought-iron fence. That's all the police needed to locate the house. While she explained all of this, the people behind her seemed to be cheering. A man in a green football jersey leaned into the camera frame and waved.

"The alleged kidnapper appears to have fled the scene," the reporter added. "Police have no description to provide at this time, but we're told that there will be a press conference later today . . ."

The news abruptly shifted to a happy story about a local dog that won first place in some Frisbee-catching contest.

"Jakmal's still out there," Ozzie said.

"So are we," Lulu replied. "Gotta be ready for next time."

"We have to do more than that," Spark said.

She was finally ready to tell them the truth about the monster, and where he really came from. When she got to the part about how the hexen betrayed Jakmal, the bears seemed ready to argue. Most likely this was the first time they heard a bear speak ill of the Founders. Yet the Grand Sleuth and its rules were so far away, and Spark stood before the juro, having risked her life, having lost her friend in battle. They had no choice but to believe her.

"Jakmal didn't keep the children in his world," she pointed out. "He kept them in ours. Maybe he thought they would be safe from other monsters here."

"Or maybe he wanted to trick them," Lulu said. "Monsters are good at that."

"I saw Matthew's cell," Spark continued. "Jakmal wasn't feeding off the boy's fear. It was almost as if the monster wanted him to feel at home. Matthew could watch all the movies he wanted. Eat blueberry waffles."

"Jakmal kidnapped your friend. There's no nice way to do that. I don't care how many waffles he gave him."

"Even so, I want to know more. I'm not sitting around and waiting for the next attack. Now, that castle had hundreds of portals stored inside. Those portals go both ways. All we have to do is find one."

"So we take the fight to him!" Lulu said.

"If it comes to that. Or we help him. If that's what it takes."

"You want to go on another adventure," Ozzie said.

"I do."

"You bears don't quit," Rana said.

They all looked at her.

"Nope," Lulu said.

"I'm sorry for what I did," Rana said.

"You came back," Spark said. "That's what you did."

Rana smiled weakly. "I'm not as brave as any of you, but I won't run away ever again."

Zed, still holding Rana's sword, waddled across the bed and handed it to the Amazon Princess. She quietly placed it in its sheath.

On the television, more updates trickled in. The reporters interviewed people who lived in the neighborhood, all of whom claimed the building was abandoned. A ticker scrolled across the bottom of the screen, displaying details about the ongoing manhunt for the kidnapper. Later, one of the news anchors gave out Matthew's name while a photo of him hung in the corner of the screen. "Matthew and his sister Loretta host a popular YouTube channel called *LM²*, or *Loretta and Matthew Love Movies!*," she said, beaming. Upon hearing that, the toys all shouted and clapped like spectators at a soccer game.

"Your dusa just picked up about ten thousand new subscribers!" Lulu said.

The clip of the dolly zoom video played, with Matthew doing his best Chief Brody impersonation as the camera zipped toward him. Then it cut to the two siblings shouting their catchphrase: "Keep dreaming, and keep trying!"

About an hour later, at the press conference, the police chief described it all as a miracle, but he could provide no information on the man who stole the children. "He must have concealed his face," the chief said. "The children could not describe him."

"Are you even sure that it was a man?" a reporter asked.

The chief fluttered his lips and shrugged. "I guess not."

Spark and her friends watched for hours, hypnotized by the television. The sun began to drop, and the family had still not returned. The tired warriors passed the time by retelling the story of battle again and again. Even Zed joined in. They compared scars, described the monster's fangs and claws. And eventually, their storytelling led to Sir Reginald. More than once, they hung their heads in silence for him.

It was around dusk when the cars returned. Doors opened and closed. Footsteps made their way to the entrance.

"Come on," Spark said. "We have to take our places."

They crept to the top of the stairs. The humans moved around the living room, oblivious to the little watchers. Matthew wore a new outfit, probably purchased that day, judging from the fresh creases in his pants. Jisha, Claire, and Darcy chatted in a corner. Several adults milled about, some yawning from the long day they endured. They were too distracted to notice the bears creeping down the hall.

Suddenly realizing that she still carried Arctos, Spark quickly shoved the sword under the rug at the top of the steps—it would be safe for now. She pointed to the recliner near the fireplace. All they needed to do was push through the bars on the railing, drop to the floor, and roll to the chair. It was close enough to where the girls left them the night before. Given all the excitement, no one would notice.

"You forgot something," Ozzie whispered to Spark.

"What's that?"

"You must release us from the juro. You have to say the words."

"Oh . . . I . . . I don't know what they are." She wanted to ask Sir Reginald. He would know.

"Room's clear," Lulu said. "Let's go. Now."

They jumped. While Rana made a thud with her heavy plastic boots, the others landed with a soft pat on the floor. They crawled to the chair and huddled close together, just another careless pile of toys.

"It's okay if you can't release us," Ozzie whispered. "We don't need to break this bond with you."

"Yeah," Lulu said. "Hey, ya never know."

"Am I in your . . . juro?" Zed asked.

"You are now," Ozzie said.

"Thank you." He turned to Rana. "And thanks for letting me use your sword."

She gripped the handle, almost as if she were reintroducing herself to it. "You used it better than I could."

"Spark," Ozzie said, "I hope your dusa really does have this power Jakmal was looking for. I know she'll put it to good use."

"That would be nice," Spark said.

She wondered again how they would face the final light, when their dusas moved on without them. She decided it did not matter. This is what they were meant to do, and it was enough.

"Thank you," Spark said. "All of you. You have my sword and my life."

"You have mine," Ozzie said.

"And mine," Zed said.

"You got mine forever," Lulu said.

A painful silence followed. In the kitchen, the phone rang.

"You all have my sword from now on," Rana said. "I swear it."

"Then you're one of us," Spark said. "Bears serve."

"Bears watch," Lulu and Ozzie said together. Soon, they were all saying it: "Bears protect. Always and forever."

Loretta came upon them a few seconds later. "Oh, here they are," she said.

THIRTY-TWO

The guests stayed late. They must have been exhausted and famished, so Mom and Dad ordered Indian food, Matthew's favorite non-waffle meal. Soon the house smelled like curry. With their bellies full, the humans began laughing and joking as if this were a typical weekend gathering. But every once in a while, the chatter would stop. Someone—Darcy's dad, or Jisha's mom, or even Claire—would make a comment about how brave Matthew had been, how strong the family was, how tough Loretta could be. And then someone would start crying, prompting others to do the same. Then someone would lighten things with a joke. It had a certain rhythm to it that made Spark smile.

As the party dispersed, each of the guests told Mom that she should call them if she needed anything. Mom thanked them, hugged them, cried some more. When the last of them left, Mom staggered into the kitchen and leaned on the table, head bowed. Dad checked the fridge. Thinking better of it, he shut the door.

On the couch, Loretta and Matthew talked about the movie.

"But why use a zoom for that shot?" Matthew asked.

"It's a dramatic moment!" Loretta said.

"You should let the scene speak for itself! You don't need all those tricks."

"I'll show it to you right now! You're gonna love it."

"No," Dad said, yawning. "Bedtime."

"Dad, you saw the shot," Loretta said. "It looks great, right?"

"Yes, of course."

"So let me show him."

"The movie isn't going anywhere," Dad said. "Show him tomorrow. You have all of spring break to work on it."

"All *right*."

Spark, still leaning on the recliner, watched as the family hugged and said good night. Mom lingered on both of the children a little longer than usual. After the children went upstairs, the parents hung their coats in the closet. Mom walked across the living room, with Dad following her. When she reached the stairs, he took her arm, twirled her around, and kissed her for a long time, until they wrapped their arms around each other. Loretta would have made fun of them if she saw it.

"I love you," Dad said.

"I love you, too."

They went upstairs. The lights switched off.

Sometime later, Spark recognized Loretta's footsteps approaching. The girl scooped her up, grabbed Zed by the tail, and carried them both to the bedroom. After setting the monkey on the bookshelf, Loretta plopped onto the mattress and draped her arm around Spark. The bear rested her head on Loretta's chest, with her paw on the girl's rib cage as it rose and fell with each breath. Loretta's eyelids fluttered, tickling Spark's fuzzy ear. Outside, the buzzing streetlamp glowed like a phony sun. The toys on the windowsill cast shadows on the rug. The house settled in, and the quietest stretch of the night began. And there were no monsters this time, only dreams.

THIRTY-THREE

The next morning, Dad opened the attic door and let out a string of curse words, several of which Spark had never heard before.

"Julie!" he shouted. "Julie, the raccoons got into the attic again!"

"What?"

"Come look!"

Spark listened. When Mom saw the attic, she repeated some of the same bad words. "How did they get in *this* time?"

"Some of the floorboards are missing."

"Oh, my God."

Loretta, still asleep, grumbled and then rolled on top of Spark. Above, Mom and Dad's footsteps clunked across the ceiling. Their muffled voices rose and fell with each discovery they made.

"Look out!" Dad said. "Raccoon!"

Mom screamed. Her feet danced as she tried to run. Dad laughed.

"You jerk!" Mom said, hitting him.

"I thought I saw one!" he said, chuckling.

For the next hour, they cleaned the mess. Loretta's room grew brighter with the rising sun. And still she slept—until Matthew knocked on her door. Rubbing her eyes, she rolled off the bed and let him in.

Spark could hardly recognize him. He seemed taller somehow. No, he merely *stood* taller. Perhaps to show that he survived whatever had happened to him, and was stronger for it.

Loretta invited him to sit beside her on the bed. "You want to talk about anything?" she asked.

He gave her a look that said, *are you kidding?* The poor boy spent the entire day before telling the same story over and over, first to the detective, then the social worker, then to a bunch of other strangers who never even introduced themselves. In the coming weeks, he would have to describe what happened many more times, to many more strangers.

"Sorry," Loretta said. "But, you know. You said you saw a monster—"

"I don't know what I saw. I swear, it feels like I dreamt the whole thing. That doctor lady says your mind can play tricks on you when you're scared."

Loretta gazed at the ceiling, worried that Mom and Dad might hear them. "Yeah, well . . . then I guess I was pretty scared. Because I saw one, too."

Matthew bit his lip.

Loretta brushed her hand against Spark's tail. "But then I felt safe again," she said. "Because I knew I wasn't alone."

Matthew nodded, his gaze drifting away from her.

"And something else happened," she said. "Last night, I heard a voice calling me. I never heard it before, but I still recognized it. Oh, God, that doesn't make any sense."

"Lots of things don't make sense."

They looked at each other. Despite all they had been through, and all that had changed, they could still say so much with a simple glance. It was a secret language that only people who grew up together could understand.

"Can't tell Mom and Dad," he said. "Not yet. I wanna know more first."

"So do I," Loretta said.

"I'm paying Sofia Lopez a visit today. After breakfast. You should come along."

"I should," she said nodding. "I got a few questions for her myself."

They sat in silence for a while, another way in which they spoke without speaking. Until finally, Matthew said, "I want to talk about something more important."

Spark stole a glance at Zed. The monkey, as usual, covered his eyes with his paws.

"I heard you put that diva Claire in her place," Matthew said.

Loretta laughed. "*I* was the diva."

Something heavy toppled over in the attic. Both the children looked at the ceiling.

"Mom and Dad are clearing things out upstairs," Matthew said. "A lot of old toys are up there. They're gonna give them to the neighbor's kids if we don't claim them."

"What?"

"Come on. Before they close the boxes."

They left. Soon there were four pairs of footsteps on the ceiling. To help pass the time, Dad dug out an ancient record player, plugged it in, and played songs by Marvin Gaye and Sam Cooke. Mom brought waffles to the attic, and they ate breakfast while sitting on boxes and dusty furniture. Spark lay on the bed and listened. The family was happy, and so was she.

"Look what I found!" Dad said.

Spark knew right away what it was. The attic went silent for a moment. Spark imagined Matthew cradling Sir Reginald while the others watched. She thought that she would cry. But still, the dusas were safe. The League of Ursus had fulfilled its mission once again.

Spark stayed in place while the children carried boxes of toys down the steps. The record player started a new song. She could not make out the words, only the *tap-tap-tap* of the cymbal.

"Spark!" Zed said. She turned to the bookshelf, but the monkey was not there. Instead, he knelt by the window, his tail flicking. The adventure last night must have given him some courage.

"What is it?" she asked.

"Come quick!"

She bounced across the bed and onto the windowsill. Outside, in the driveway, she saw Matthew holding a box of toys and stuffed animals. Sir Reginald lay on top of the pile, his glassy eyes facing the sky. Matthew spoke to Jared, the little boy from next door. The boy stood with his hands folded, listening intently.

Spark shuddered at the sight of it. She wanted to pound on the glass. She wanted to leap from the window and land on the asphalt and tell Matthew to stop what he was doing.

"We have to do something!" Zed said.

The options raced through her mind. They could throw an object to distract them. Or she could swing down on a string. She had become quite the expert in that recently. Or—yes, this would work!—she would break into the neighbor's house in the dead of night and steal Sir Reginald back. Zed wouldn't like it. She knew what he would say. But it was the only way.

Matthew handed the box over to Jared. The smaller boy almost tipped over when he took it. And then Matthew swiped Sir Reginald from the pile and held him at arm's length. He pulled the bear to his chest and squeezed him hard. He whispered something that only he and Sir Reginald could hear. Finally, he set him gently in the box and patted the bear's head. Jared said thank you and headed for his house. Matthew waved. He was only twelve years old, and yet he was a boy no longer. The old bear had helped him along this path.

Spark's sense of panic lifted. A wave of joy washed over her, unlike anything she had ever felt before. This was what Sir Reginald wanted. This is what they all lived for.

"It's okay," Spark said. "Let him go."

Zed whimpered. Spark shushed him. She concentrated on Sir Reginald as Jared carted him away. At the last possible moment, right before Jared rounded the corner and disappeared, Spark swore she saw the old bear tilt his head ever so slightly, with a slight twitch of the left eye that could have been a wink, to let her know that everything would be all right.

"Did you see that?" she asked.

"See what?"

She reached out and took Zed's hand in her paw. "Hey, monkey. Don't be afraid."

"I'm not afraid. I'm sad."

He started to cry. Spark squeezed his hand.

"We don't know what Sir Reginald said to Matthew when he found him," she said. "Maybe he told the boy to do this. So the bear could find a new friend to protect. He goes where he's needed, remember?"

"But isn't he . . . dead?"

"I don't know. He said it was a child's love that brought us here. Maybe it can bring us back."

The monkey could not understand. Spark would keep trying anyway.

"There's something else Sir Reginald always told me," she said. "Things change. Things move on."

Beside her, Zed sniffled.

"But that's a *good* thing," she added. "It means we did our job."

Someone was approaching. Without a word, they returned to their places. Zed to the bookshelf, Spark to the bed. Loretta entered the room, a wistful smile on her face. She changed into jeans and a T-shirt, leaving her pajamas in a heap on the floor.

Downstairs, Matthew called her name a few times. "Are you ready or what?"

"Yeah, hold on!" As she slung her purse over her shoulder, she flicked Zed's tail. Then she tapped Spark's head with her fingers before walking out.

The house was still, and quiet. And safe. Spark, being a good bear, kept her eyes open for any signs of trouble.

Acknowledgments

I am eternally grateful to the many people who helped bring this book to life.

I start, as always, by thanking my tireless agent, Jennifer Weltz, who has been a champion of my work since 2012. Her patience and guidance have made me a better writer.

I also want to thank my editor, Rebecca Gyllenhaal, who led this book apart and put it back together again, a true literary feat of strength. Her dedication is a superpower. I also thank the entire staff at Quirk Books, who are so good at taking a goofy story like mine and creating something that can be shared with the world. In particular, I would like to thank Katherine McGuire, Jane Morley, Jhanteigh Kupihea, and Brett Cohen, among many others.

I'm lucky to be part a writing community made up mostly of my friends from Emerson College, several of whom are now scattered about the country. Ashley Wells has had to listen to stories of this project for years now, and I am so grateful for her generosity, support, and insight. My friends Jane Berentson, Brian Hurley, Michelle Lipinski, Allison Trzop, Mike Moats, and Cam Terwilliger are also permanent members of my juro.

My parents Nick and Loretta let my brother and me watch (almost) any movie we wanted, which is probably what brought me here. When I was a child, Friday night at the Repino household usually involved a rented VHS tape, a pizza, and my mom asking why the action heroes have to use such bad language. Thank you so much.

About The Author

Nicholas Repino

ROBERT REPINO is the author of *Mort(e)*, *Culdesac*, and *D'Arc*, which make up the critically acclaimed War with No Name series (Soho Press). He holds an MFA in creative writing from Emerson College and teaches at the Gotham Writers' Workshop. By day, he's an editor at Oxford University Press. This is his middle-grade debut. He lives in New York City.

Growing up, Robert had two special teddy bears: Bear and Blue Bear.